Center for Basque Studies
Basque Literature Series, No. 1

BASQUE LITERATURE SERIES

An Anthology of Basque Short Stories

Compiled by MARI JOSE OLAZIREGI

Basque Literature Series Editors
Mari Jose Olaziregi and Linda White

Center for Basque Studies,
University of Nevada, Reno

Center for Basque Studies
Basque Literature Series, No. 1

Center for Basque Studies
University of Nevada, Reno
Reno, Nevada 89557
http://basque.unr.edu

Library of Congress Cataloging-in-Publication Data

An anthology of Basque short stories / compiled by Mari Jose Olaziregi ;
[edited by Linda White ; translated by Kristin Addis ... [et al.].
    p. cm. -- (Basque literature series ; no. 1)
    Includes bibliographical references.
    ISBN 1-877802-40-9 (pbk.) -- ISBN 1-877802-41-7 (hardcover)
    1. Short stories, Basque--Translations into English. 2. Basque
fiction--20th century--Translations into English. I. Olaziregi, Mari
Jose. II. White, Linda, 1949- III. Addis, Kristin. IV. Title. V. Series.

    PH5397.E8A56 2004
    899'.92--dc22

2004014872

TRANSLATED BY

Kristin Addis
Amaia Gabantxo
Margaret Jull Costa
Elizabeth Macklin
Linda White

Foreword (written by Mari Jose Olaziregi)
Translated by Kristin Addis

Bernardo Atxaga's "Teresa, *poverina mia*"
Translated by Margaret Jull Costa

Harkaitz Cano's "The Mattress"
Translated by Elizabeth Macklin and Linda White

Javi Cillero Goiriastuena's "A Kiss in the Dark"
Translated by Amaia Gabantxo

Juan Garzia Garmendia's "Gubbio"
Translated by Kristin Addis

Arantxa Iturbe's "Maria and Jose" and "The Red Shawl"
Translated by Amaia Gabantxo

Anjel Lertxundi's "Berlin Is Not So Far Away"
Translated by Amaia Gabantxo

Karlos Linazasoro's "The Derailment"
Translated by Amaia Gabantxo

Pello Lizarralde's "Awkward Silence"
Translated by Elizabeth Macklin and Linda White

Xabier Montoia's "Black as Coal"
Translated by Kristin Addis

Inazio Mujika Iraola's "Like the Waters Release Their Dead"
Translated by Kristin Addis

Lourdes Oñederra's "Mrs Anderson's Longing"
Translated by Amaia Gabantxo

Ixiar Rozas' "A Draft"
Translated by Elizabeth Macklin and Linda White

Joseba Sarrionandia's "Alone," "The Treasure Chest," and
    "The Ancient Mariner"
Translated by Linda White
Biographical note translated by Kristin Addis

Iban Zaldua's "Bibliography" and "Invisible Friend"
Translated by Kristin Addis

Texts edited by Linda White

CONTENTS

Acknowledgments

Translation of these stories was made possible by funding from the Basque Government, in collaboration with the Ministry of Education, Universities and Research, the Ministry of Culture, and the Secretary General of Foreign Affairs.

FOREWORD

by Mari Jose Olaziregi

translated by Kristin Addis

As they say, an anthology is usually the result of error since, even with the best of intentions, the selection of stories always poses the risk of committing obvious omission. Things get even thornier with an invitation to contribute a foreword to an anthology, since if there's anything we love as readers, it's to sit right down and dig into the stories. Without a doubt, the stories are the important thing in the book, and we would like to begin by stressing that, as R. Ford[1] writes in a foreword of his own, reading the stories makes more sense than anything that could be said in a foreword. With this in mind, we will try to be clear and concise, to choose our words aptly, as in good stories.

Although we know that every literature gives rise to the dialogue between the particular and the universal, few Basque authors have managed to cross borders; for too long a time, few Basque authors have managed to make their voices heard in the canon of the monochromatic and monological panorama of Western literature. One of these few is Bernardo Atxaga, whose book *Obabakoak* (1988, published in English under the same title) can now

---

[1] Ford, R. (ed.) *Antología del cuento norteamericano* (Barcelona: Galaxia Gutemberg & Círculo de Lectores, 2002).

be read in 25 languages; in it he proposes a new cartography with which to brave geographical and literary frontiers: "These days nothing can be said to be peculiar to one place or person. The world is everywhere and Euskal Herria is no longer just Euskal Herria but (…) 'the place where the world takes the name of Euskal Herria'." [2]

To understand this map splashed with the physical geography of Basque, English readers can turn to Mark Kurlansky's *The Basque History of the World* [3] in which the outsider will find many fascinating details about us: we speak Basque, the oldest Western European language, a language with only 700,000 speakers in all; our country measures only 8,218 square miles, a plot of land a little smaller than New Hampshire; this territory is divided between Spain and France but as Kurlansky states, "Basqueland looks too green to be Spain and too rugged to be France" (p. 18). Additionally, a number of instances in which the adjective "euskal" is featured are specifically mentioned: the fame of our cuisine (the preparation and conservation of codfish, for example); our well-known sport, jai alai (Basque handball); our most famous religious figure, Saint Ignatius of Loyola; our excellent Basque sculptors J. Oteiza and E. Chillida; the Guggenheim Museum of Bilbao… and the provocative issue of terrorism, considered to be the biggest problem for the 2.4 million people living in the Basque Country. As Kurlansky's book reminds us, terrorism is the topic of fully 85% of articles published in the United States on

---

[2] Bernardo Atxaga, *Obabakoak*, trans. Margaret Jull Costa, (New York: Vintage, 1994), p. 324.

[3] Mark Kurlansky, *The Basque History of the World*, (New York: Penguin, 2001).

Basque issues. We cannot deny that this harsh reality fundamentally colors our lives and thus it naturally appears in some of the stories in this anthology (Iban Zaldua's powerful story *Bibliography*, for example). Among other things, because this is one of the purposes of literature: to exorcise demons, whether those of an individual or of a people. Literature of whatever genre is more truthful than either media reports or the official story given in history texts. This goal, that is, the discovery of truth, was considered by Edgar Allan Poe to be a characteristic of the short story and, if we accept this view, the reader will find in this anthology more than a few Basque truths. These truths question our fears, raise our ghosts, tell our dreams or, as André Gide would have it, recount our miseries.

And the writers in this anthology present these questions in Basque, in our ancient language of pre-Indo-European origin. Basque (Euskara) gives its name and its nature to our country, Euskal Herria, the land of Euskara speakers, and for that reason we have tried, despite its historical prohibition, despite its problems, to hold tight to our language through the centuries. In the final analysis, as G. Steiner reminds us, when a language dies, a way of understanding the world dies with it, a way of looking at the world. One way of holding onto our language and crossing borders is to win new readers through translation. But borders, though a spur to literary creativity in the opinion of Claudio Magris, are a heavy burden for Basques. Thus few of our writers have managed to put us on the map in foreign countries and, though nowadays Basque reaches 87 million homes in Europe and 3 million families in the United States thanks to radio and television, no such thing has happened with Basque books.

One of the writers in this anthology, Harkaitz Cano, paraphrasing Auden's *Letters from Iceland*, compares the situation of our literature to the solitude of an island, an old European island, nevertheless often visited by well-known authors thanks to translation – it is a pleasure to be able to read Joyce, Faulkner, Eliot, Chekhov, Carver in Basque – but from whose shores few excursions to foreign territory have been made. In total, only 60 titles have been translated from Basque to other languages, doubtless too few for a nation of such dedicated travelers.

The socio-historical situation of Basque is the cause of the rather late evolution of our literature. From 1545, when the first Basque book was published, Bernard Etxepare's *Linguae Vasconum Primitiae*, to 1879, only some 100 books were published in Basque. Numbers began to rise at the beginning of the 20th century, when Basque literature began to gain strength; only then, in B. Atxaga's metaphor, did the hedgehog creep out of his hiding place. [4] In a brief review of 20th-century Basque literature, we find the post-symbolic poets Lizardi and Lauaxeta in the 1930s; in the 50s and 60s, the Bilbaino Gabriel Aresti, an excellent representative of social poetry; and in the 60s new novelists who revisited and remodeled the typical late 19th century novel (Txillardegi, for example, was a follower of Sartre and Camus, and Ramon Saizarbitoria brought experimentalism to the Basque novel). Nevertheless, if there is any critical event in the history of Basque literature, it is the death of the dictator Franco in 1975. Only then did Basque literature begin to establish the conditions necessary for its development (the bilin-

---

[4] See prologue to Bernardo Atxaga's *Obabakoak* (no page number in Vintage edition).

gual decree, which expanded the corpus of potential readers, official funding for publishers and distributors, funding to protect production in Basque...). Nowadays, of the 1500 books published every year in Basque, approximately 14% are literature, and among these, narrative is prominent at 60% of all published literature. [5] But though this may be true, it's the novel that holds the central place in our modern literature; in ours, as in other literatures, the market is a controlling factor and the most profitable genre, the novel, therefore triumphs.

This anthology is thus rather daring in that we have chosen the short story, a genre that arose late in our literary development, to launch this *Basque Literature Series*. The reasons are evident. First, an anthology provides the opportunity to introduce several of our 300 Basque writers. Here, the reader will discover the most fundamental characteristics that define our contemporary narrative: the pluralism of our generation and our esthetic tendencies. Additionally, our objective is the English-speaking audience, among whom the short story has enjoyed long tradition and recognition; we believe that for this reason, this is an apt genre with which to begin the series. The welcome that the short story receives in the English-speaking world has always been cause for envy among modern Basque writers, whether from the Spanish or French Basque Country, since they typically receive little attention from literary institutions. Not only because the initial theoretical formulation that established the origin

---

[5] As the body of Basque literature becomes stronger, narrative has gained a greater and greater prominence. Thus, while narrative held only 18.7% of literary publication from 1876 to 1935, it rose to 23.8% between 1936 and 1975, and today, as stated, accounts for more than half of all Basque literary publication.

of modern short story ("literary story," "tale") originated in America (see the works of Poe), but also because of the evolution of the genre itself in the 20th century. In the 1980s, both our literature and Spanish literature experienced a revival of the short story, the reasons for which can be found not only in the example provided in the works of various well-known South American authors (Quiroga, Borges and Cortázar, for example), but also in the influence of contemporary US writers (beginning with Cheever and leading up to Carver, Wolff and Ford, said to be representatives of minimalism). Basque writers now saw themselves in this new light and, even though the last two decades have been very interesting in the short story, we are still far from definitive socio-literary acclaim in what Faulkner considered "the most demanding form after poetry." [6]

Our intention was to produce an anthology of recent Basque stories and, although there are a couple of stories from the 1980s (there are always exceptions), all the rest were originally published in the 1990s. Furthermore, we did not seek a balance in either style or theme; the quality of the stories, in our opinion, inspired us and was the overriding principle in including them in this anthology. And on the topic of quality, we would like to add here that we sought the characteristics that Carver and Jenks required of the stories in their anthology, that is "stories which on occasion had the ambition of enlarging our view of ourselves and the world."[7] Together with the sto-

---

[6] J. B. Meriwether and M. Millgate, *Lion in the Garden: Interviews with William Faulkner 1926-1962* (Lincoln: Nebraska University Press, 1968), p. 238.

[7] W. L. Stull, ed., *No Heroics, Please. Uncollected Writings* (London, Harvill Press, 1991), p. 147.

ries, we include the bio-bibliographies that we requested of our writers. The reader will readily perceive that these short introductory texts written by the authors bring out the ties that their stories have with life's mysteries, questions and rifts. In the end, this literary genre which entails concentration, tension and illumination seeks only to captivate the reader so that the stories enter into his/her own biography and remain there at least a short time. With this in mind, the present anthology includes not only authors who have written only (or primarily) books of short stories (Cillero, Garzia, Iturbe, Linazasoro, Lizarralde, Mujika Iraola, Zaldua), but also those who have made interesting contributions to other literary genres (Atxaga, Cano, Lertxundi, Montoia, Oñederra, Rozas, Sarrionandia)… In other words, those with an extensive bibliography together with those whose journey has so far been shorter. Finally, there is one more aspect of the chosen texts that deserves comment: their length. Although most of these stories are approximately the same length (most are under 15 pages), we have included some interesting writers who have written truly short stories. In their case, we have chosen more than one story; from a literary point of view this might seem a dubious practice, but we hope the reader will understand our wish to provide some sort of balance.

The short story, this autonomous modern genre of adult literature and its craft, is a new phenomenon in Basque literature. A. Lertxundi's *Hunik arrats artean* (1970, *Wait Until Dusk*) is considered to be the first fruit of modern Basque short story. In it, we see the notable effects on narrative of both South American magic realism and the theater of the absurd (García Márquez, Rulfo; Kafka, Artaud). Other Basque collections of stories published in the 1970s adopted traditional models from folk tales or the experimentation that was then prevalent in novels. In any case, the 1980s were without a doubt a decade of strengthening and expansion in modern Basque short story. In our country as well as in others, the proliferation of literary journals did much to promote narrative, but in our case, the political situation from 1975 on facilitated funding, literary prizes and the campaign for literacy. In 1978, the literary group POTT Banda (pott = failure) was formed in Bilbao, opening new literary universes to contemporary Basque narrative. Members included Bernardo Atxaga, Joseba Sarrionandia and Joxemari Iturralde, who in the 1980s published works that would change the panorama of Basque narrative. The members of POTT looked to the English-language literary tradition (crime novels, the cinema, adventure fiction, etc.), and the works of J. L. Borges provided the essential path toward this tradition, the universal inheritance found in his labyrinthine library. Joseba Sarrionandia's *Narrazioak* (1983, *Narrations*) and Bernardo Atxaga's *Obabakoak* (1988) are considered to be POTT Banda's most illustrious contributions to the contemporary Basque short story.

Very slowly, from the 1980s onward, the typology of the Basque story became richer and richer and, as in the novel, today's panorama is truly eclectic. Adopting the characteristics that define this multi-faceted modernity, modern Basque short stories feature realism presented from an expressionist point of view, fantasy in the style of Cortázar or Borges (also known as neofantasy), metafiction, tales of a lyrical tone rooted in the past, stories that speak to us of the absurdity of life, minimalist accounts of daily life, hybridity... But above all, today's Basque narrative has abandoned the experimentalism of the 1970s in favor of the simple desire to tell stories and, especially among the writers of the 90s, the influence of the cinema, music and the media is ever more obvious. Finally, it is accepted that reality is like broken glass and that it is up to the reader to rearrange the pieces. In the same way, the new hybrid stories, which break through the frontiers of the genre, demand a new type of dialogue with the reader, either through collections which propose new structures or ties between stories (such as in a short story cycle), or through almost chronicle- or essay-like fiction.

In 1983, the successful *Narrazioak* was published, **Joseba Sarrionandia**'s first book of short stories. In poetic prose of enticing images and metaphors, the author shows his fondness for fantasy and ancient legends; the reader will find sirens and ancient mariners (betraying Sarrionandia's fascination with Coleridge and Melville), characters who do homage to the legend of King Arthur: Queen Ginebra, Sir Galahad... solitary stopping-points, and a meditation on literature, in other words, metaliterature. The reader will find one of the ancient mariners of *Narrazioak* in this anthology, as well as in the short-short stories from *Han izanik hona naiz* (1992, *Having Been There, Here I Am*) and *Miopeak, bizikletak eta beste langabetu batzuk* (1995, *Myopic People, Bicycles and Other Redundancies*) In the latter, the hybridity that is characteristic of Sarrionandia's work is evident, as is his desire to break through the restrictions of the genre. Putting a new spin on stories taken from both the literary and oral traditions, playing with black humor and irony, Sarrionandia in his short stories brings to mind the supershort texts of writers like A. Monterroso.

As mentioned above, **Bernardo Atxaga**'s *Obabakoak* (1988) was a milestone in contemporary Basque literature and, as Anjel Lertxundi (one of the writers included in this anthology) confirms, things were never the same in Basque literature after it. The author presents a collection of short stories with an innovative structure, one that binds ancient Basque superstitions to postmodern examination of literature. International criticism has defined *Obabakoak* as an intertextual voyage that begins with *The Thousand and One Nights* and continues with the master storytellers of the 19ᵗʰ and 20ᵗʰ centuries (Chekhov, Waugh, Maupassant, Villiers de l'Isle-Adam, Borges, Cortázar and Calvino were, among others, Atxaga's fellow-travelers). On this voyage, the writer speaks to us of the boundaries between literature and life and of the conflict between nature and civilization, using the techniques of fantastic literature for that purpose. And there is fear in the foundation of that fantasy for, as R. Callois and others have defined it, fantastic literature plays with fear. In the story chosen for this anthology, *Teresa, Poverina Mia*, Atxaga again investigates human fears and desires and, as in the novels *The Lone Man* (Harvill, 1996) and *The Lone Woman* (Harvill, 1999), to invoke M. Montaigne, we delve into the internal and bellicose world of the protagonist. The story's lyrical tone stands out and, as in Chekhov's stories, the author's repeated images and metaphors take root inside us.

The poetic prose of **Inazio Mujika Iraola** likewise has a truly lyrical tone. In his 1987 book *Azukrea belazeetan* (*Sugar on the Prairie*), we see the influence of South

American magic realism and particularly that of J. Rulfo. This type of realism is captivating, not only in many neoruralist Basque novels of the time, but also in other short stories worthy of mention (I. Zurutuza's 1989 story *Haizeak iparlaino beltzak dakartzanean, When the wind brings the cold northern fog*, for example), and the fantasy found in Basque oral tradition put us in the limelight. This narrative makes possible a way of visiting our past, a way of recapturing an identity denied us for years. And given that memory has become the primary obsession of modern Basque novelists (see Ramon Saizarbitoria's *Gorde nazazu lurpean* (2002, *Leave Me In the Earth*), for example), it is no surprise to see the importance of memory in the works of Mujika Iraola. The fiction that arises from mixing legends and Borgesian expertise is the basis of his collection of stories *Hautsaren Kronika* (1994, *Chronicle of Dust*). In the story we chose for this anthology, *Like the waters release their dead*, dramatic memories from the time of WWII rise to the surface, very slowly.

The past is similarly recovered in two other short stories in this anthology. In **Javi Cillero**'s story *A kiss in the dark*, from *Hollywood eta biok* (1998, *Hollywood and Me*), for example, the point of departure is a flashback to adolescence. *Hollywood eta biok* reflects the influence of US cinema and narrative and in it, the reader will find stories that vary in length and structure, told in Cillero's unornamented prose with humor, irony and skill. **Xabier Montoia** also turns to the past in his book *Gasteizko hondartzak* (1997, *The Beaches of Gasteiz*). Though in his last two novels, this author also revisits the different moments and epochs of our history, Montoia's narrative goal is not to bear historical witness. The characteristics of dirty realism also appear in his collection of stories *Emakume biboteduna* (1992, *The Mustachioed Woman*), for example, in which he presents sharp and realistic stories based on love or the lack of love, and which are echoed in the provocative nature of M. Duchamp's painting on the cover. The stories in *Baina bihotzak dio* (2002, *But the Heart Says*), on the other hand, focus on homesickness for the Basque Country but, above and beyond this, Montoia offers us the chance to see the world through the eyes of his believable characters. Credibility and intensity are conspicuous in the story we chose for this anthology, *Black as coal*. This, the first of the twenty-two short stories of *Gasteizko hondartzak*, opens in the town of Gasteiz (Vitoria) at the end of the 1960s. The history of the city passes before our eyes as the backdrop to the lively cast of characters who appear and disappear from story to story.

Like Montoia's stories, the works by Arantxa Iturbe, Harkaitz Cano and Iban Zaldua which we have included in this anthology are firmly based in realism. **Arantxa Iturbe**, one of the not quite 11% of Basque writers who are women, published lively short stories on love and the lack of it in her books *Ezer baino lehen* (1992, *Before Anything Else*) and *Lehenago zen berandu* (1995, *It Was Late Before*). The principle characters are women, urban women living in today's media-infested and stressful society. Iturbe bases her spirited, spontaneous and colloquial stories on everyday life and on misunderstandings with men. **Harkaitz Cano**'s realist narrative, on the other hand, is quite different. Black novels written in the rhythm of jazz or blues, poetry books sprinkled with Basquiat, Boris Vian, Maiakovski, Carver and famous movie directors, Cano's chronicles show that he is a dedicated student of Capote. Such is his literary universe: a desolate modern city, anonymous telephone calls and abandoned streets, bits of stories that speak to us of the lack of love are all found in his minimalist stories. Cano's book *Telefono kaiolatua* (1997, *The Caged Telephone*), from which we have chosen the story *The mattress*, includes elements both black and absurd. As in the short stories of the masters Chekhov and Carver, humble elements and details report on the protagonist's inner life, with compelling comparisons and metaphors in which to delight. The old and stained mattress which serves as an x-ray of the protagonists' lives, or the agreements which function as premonitions, situate us in a story in which apparently little happens.

Few are the Basque storytellers who have mastered the short-short story as well as **Iban Zaldua**. Borges' or Calvino's metaliterary stance, or Cortázar's shocking fantasy, among other things, serve as the point of departure for Zaldua's pointed, ironic and humorous stories. And this writer uses his critical scrutiny to fragment topics such as literature, life and Basque reality. Hence, the meaningful titles of his books: *Gezurrak, gezurrak, gezurrak* (2000, *Lies, Lies, Lies*) or *Traizioak* (2001, *Betrayals*). Zaldua has shown that he is capable of writing in rich registers and styles, shaping his stories without a single extraneous word. Because of their intensity, Zaldua's short stories will never leave the reader cold; for Zaldua the short story is, as J. Cheever says, what we tell ourselves in the unequivocal moment of death.

The existential anguish caused by death is very much present in the work of **Karlos Linazasoro**. This anguish appears in his stories under the guise of the literature of the absurd (echoes of Kafka and the theater of the absurd), and is expressed in the upside-down fantasy of irrational logic (Cortázar). The mixture of reality and dream, the suffocating atmosphere, delirium, savagery... these are the elements of Linazasoro's tales. This explains why there are so many crazy people in his stories, because they depict the irrationality behind the mask. We chose the story for this anthology, *The derailment*, from the second of his four collections of short stories, *Ez balego beste mundurik* (2000, *If There Wasn't Another World*). To the reader it will seem a surrealist and brutal story of a person reading Cioran while traveling on a train, and we are certain that he will find the comparisons and frightening scenes disturbing.

The slippery borders between literature and life are subject to debate in metafiction. Tempering the difference between fiction and essay, presenting the status of writing as a collage, metafiction makes us recognize that everything has already been said and that all writing is rewriting. J. L. Borges' Library of Babel or I. Calvino's literary artefacts are much in evidence in several of the stories of Anjel Lertxundi and Juan Garzia. **Anjel Lertxundi**, who in 1970 wrote the first modern Basque collection of short stories, is one of the most prolific writers in Basque literature. If anything defines his narrative (ten novels, four collections of short stories...) it is relentless scrutiny, the exploration of different literary means of expression. Metafiction has always been present in his work, but it is particularly so in his book of stories, *Urtero da aurten* (1984, *Yearly Means This Year*) and in the novel *Argizariaren egunak* (1997, *Days of Wax*). In the story we chose for this anthology, *Berlin is not so far away*, the 15th-century artist Jean Foquet's painting *Madonna and Child* is the point of departure for an amazing story. This fiction based on true historical events is a reflection on the ties between art and reality, and Lertxundi asks us if works of art must swallow and make disappear the real references used in their construction. **Juan Garzia** has translated into Basque Shakespeare, Melville, Beckett and J. L. Borges among others, and *Itzalen itzal* (1993, *Shadow of Shadows*) is his strongest collection of short stories. In it, we find eleven chapters and a scrap of conversation (Borgesian), but we cannot say that this is a loose collection of stories, because they gather themselves into a wholeness. One of these stories is *Gubbio*, chosen for this anthology. It tells the disturbing story of a 13th-century nun, her transgression (blasphemy) and its dramatic consequences. Citing dubious sources, making reference to apocryphal books, reaping humor and the absurd... Garzia's work teaches us that literature can be an interesting game. As the critic Iñaki Aldekoa states, shadow is everything, convention is everything in this book of Garzia's.

The next two authors in this anthology play with looks and glances. In **Lourdes Oñederra**'s stories, both in her novel *Eta emakumeari sugeak esan zion* (1999, *And the Snake Told the Woman*) and in the story *Mrs. Anderson's longing*, it is a look that makes desire evident. Because the subject of Oñederra's short story is the desire of an aging woman, she mentions Doris Lessing's *Love, Again* at the beginning. Glances, short and interrupted sentences, repeated names and elements that mark the rhythm, sensual descriptions... these are the components of Oñederra's work, especially the measured prose that plays with silence, the gaps and breaks that seek the reader's participation. In her short story *Korronteak* (*Currents*), **Ixiar Rozas** looks outside in order to look inside. The short stories in *Sartu, korrontea dabil* (2001, *Come In, There's a Draft*) have unusual ties and create a structure almost like that of a novel. We have chosen the first story in this collection, *A draft, a current*, in which one senses Rozas' humane regard that nonetheless is as cold as a movie camera. This writer who admires John Berger has said many times that she learned to look from English-language writers, learned to see the invisible creatures (immigrants, the ostracized...) that are lost in big cities. The passing glances of characters who don't know each other are captured by a meaningful gesture and recounted in the present, the currents that expand or reduce the gaps between these characters.

The writer **Pello Lizarralde**'s story *Awkward Silence* completes this anthology. His is a minimalist prose that plays with silence, that knows how to create a truly strange atmosphere. And in the recently published novel *Larrepetit* (2002) we find the characters fleeing in endless comings and goings. The reader will soon note that few things "happen" in Lizarralde's stories and that he inevitably draws the attention of the narrator to gestures, smells, colors and ordinary motions of almost epiphanic meaning. Making use of descriptions of great lyrical force, raising the objectives of different methods of storytelling to new pinnacles, the atmosphere, the internal life is dominant in Lizarralde's narrative. The same talent for creating moods that he showed in his book *Sargori* (1994, *Heat Wave*) is present in this work as well.

We conclude with a quote from W. Benjamin which expresses our hopes for the stories in this anthology: "a story stays in the memory and compels the listener to tell it to someone." Amen.

I write in a strange language. Its verbs,
the structure of its relative clauses,
the words it uses to designate ancient things
– rivers, plants, birds –
have no sisters anywhere on Earth.
A house is *etxe*, a bee *erle*, death *heriotz*.
The sun of the long winters we call *eguzki* or *eki*;
the sun of the sweet, rainy springs is also
– as you'd expect – called *eguzki* or *eki*.
(it's a strange language, but not that strange).

Born, they say, in the megalithic age,
it survived, this stubborn language, by withdrawing,
by hiding away like a hedgehog in a place,
which, thanks to the traces it left behind there,
the world named the Basque Country or *Euskal Herria*.
Yet its isolation could never have been absolute
– cat is *katu*, pipe is *pipa*, logic is *lojika* –
rather, as the prince of detectives would have said,
the hedgehog, my dear Watson, crept out of its hiding place
(to visit, above all, Rome and all its progeny).

The language of a tiny nation, so small
you cannot even find it on the map,
it never strolled in the gardens of the Court
or past the marble statues of government buildings;
in four centuries it produced only a hundred books...
the first in 1545; the most important in 1643;
the Calvinist New Testament in 1571;
the complete Catholic Bible around 1860.
Its sleep was long, its bibliography brief
(but in the twentieth century, the hedgehog awoke).

BERNARDO ATXAGA
(in Atxaga, B., *Obabakoak*, London: Hutchinson, 1992)

BERNARDO ATXAGA (1951, Asteasu)

Bernardo Atxaga has been a professional writer for over twenty years and, during that time, he has published poetry, novels, short stories, children's literature, as well as hybrid texts that play with the boundaries between essay and fiction. However, the book that has garnered the most praise and the most awards internationally is *Obabakoak* (1988), which has now been translated into 25 languages. With this book, Atxaga demonstrated that terms like 'peripheral' or 'minority literature' need be no barrier to a Basque writer or, put another way, he has shown that it is possible to be both universal and genuinely Basque. (M. J. Olaziregi)

Teresa, *poverina mia*

by

BERNARDO ATXAGA

Translated by Margaret Jull Costa

Teresa had something wrong with her right knee,
which meant that she had a slight limp, a fact that
had been the cause of great sorrow to her ever since she
was an adolescent. Although there was nothing very
noticeable about the way she walked, and although, with
time, her body had grown pretty and her face, 'with the
golden eyes of a goat,' had become particularly attractive,
she was unable to rid her memory of the words which
– on 12 August 1978, her fourteenth birthday – had
emerged from the mouth of an Italian tourist who was a
regular guest at her parents' boarding house: 'Teresa,
poverina mia!' Those three words had been spoken with
such feeling, sympathy and pity, that Teresa – finding a
new, darker meaning to the mocking remarks made by
classmates and by her playmates on the beach, and suddenly fully aware of her situation – burst into incon-
solable tears, just as, when a jug shatters, the water spills
out onto the floor. When those around her asked what
was wrong – her mother, if her knee was hurting; her
brother (two years older than her), if her tears were due
to the excitement of the moment and the fact that she
was still a silly little girl; her father (glancing at the Italian woman who spent every summer at the boarding

house), if this was any way to behave with their friend and guest, Signora di Castri, making such a fuss; Aunt Magdalena (looking angrily at her father and at the others), if she felt like going away and never seeing any of them ever again – she spoke of a school friend who had drowned in the sea that spring after slipping on the rocks below the jetty, and who, had she lived, would also have been fourteen, and how when she had thought of her, she had all of a sudden felt terribly cold and that this was the reason for her tears. They all accepted or pretended to accept this explanation and went out onto the balcony with the slices of cake hurriedly handed round by Aunt Magdalena. There were lovely views from the balcony: you could see the jetty, part of the beach, and beyond it, the blue of the sea.

That night, Teresa added a new chapter to the five – entitled 'The Boarding House,' 'The Workshop,' 'My Parents,' 'Aunt Magdalena' and 'My Brother' – that appeared in her secret diary, and at the top of the page, she wrote Signora di Castri's words: Teresa, *poverina mia!* Teresa devoted four pages to analyzing the problem of her lameness from a point of view which was intended to be totally objective. She should not feel resentful towards Signora di Castri, but, on the contrary, she should be grateful to her for revealing so clearly, in just three words, the true extent of her misfortune. It was true, there was no hope. Because of her disability, she would have to renounce many of the good things in life. Love, of course, would be denied her. She had already noticed that the boys at school took no notice of her or, if they did, it was only in order to make fun or to play cruel jokes. But what did that matter? Wasn't the misfortune of the girl who had slipped on the rocks and drowned in the sea far greater? Besides, if things got worse, she could always take that way out – wait until the tide was in, climb down into one of the gaps in the jetty and let herself slip into the sea.

Fifteen years later, this melodramatic confession in her diary was almost forgotten, but not Signora di Castri's words. These continued to live in some fold in her brain, and sometimes, like a nagging refrain, like the cricket's song as it moves its wings in the darkness of its nest, they would suddenly appear in her thoughts – Teresa, *poverina mia!* – with exactly the same pitying tone and intention of fifteen years before; it could be anywhere, at any time: when she was having a shower, going through some invoices at work, or when she was sitting on one of the benches along the jetty, smoking her last cigarette of the day. At such moments, her mind noticed what she described in her diary as 'a resurgence of the message,' and she dreamed of being able 'to drive away once and for all' the cricket that had crawled inside her when she was fourteen; although, sometimes, with barely contained sarcasm, she would forget about the anxiety provoked by this memory and would, instead, admire its durability, its vividness and perpetual freshness, qualities notable by their absence in the other chapter titles in her diary. These – 'The Boarding House,' 'The Workshop,' etc. – had lost their real meaning and were now like entries in an antiquated dictionary, sad voices, names that spoke of the precariousness of life. The boarding house, for example, the seven-room house in which she and her brother had been born, was now a modern hotel with two hundred bedrooms. As for the workshop, the place in the Old Harbor where Aunt Magdalena once repaired the fishermen's clothes and nets, had become one of a chain of cafés. 'We'll show them we're no fools, Teresa,' her aunt had said to her on the day when Teresa had been told she would inherit the workshop. 'As soon as I reach retirement age, and I no longer have to work for the fishermen, we'll take all this junk and throw it in the sea. Then we'll talk to some big company about setting up a restaurant here or a café, and ask for twenty per cent of the profits in exchange for the site. We might as well take advantage of being in the Old Harbor. It's a favorite spot for tourists to come and sit.' And that is exactly what they had done.

The changes to Aunt Magdalena's workshop and to her parents' boarding house had, ultimately, been positive ones. True, she had left behind part of her life so that some truck could come and carry it off to the dump, along with the chipped partition walls and the broken-down furniture; on the other hand, that loss had put her in a most unusual economic position, one that allowed her to be different. For, thanks to her money, she, who knew she was different – irredeemably, eternally different – had found another more gratifying way of demonstrating this difference, in the way that she dressed and adorned herself. She didn't wear a lot of jewellery, but what she did wear was always of exceptional quality. She got through about forty outfits a year and had an amazing collection of shoes. 'You've got a real treasure house stashed away in your wardrobes and drawers. Aren't you forgetting that true beauty comes from within?' her brother said mockingly when they were still living with their father in an apartment on one of the top floors of the hotel. But she was immune to such remarks. Even the word 'brother' was no longer what it once was. It lacked the glow it had had in the early pages of her diary.

'Some years ago, when I was still a little girl,' said the
entry for 2 September 1977, 'I saw a little orange bottle
near the stone steps of the harbor and I went down the
steps to try and catch it. But the water kept carrying it
just out of reach. Then my brother appeared and, when
he saw what was happening, he jumped into the water,
got the bottle and swam back to me with it. It wasn't
worth anything, it was just a discarded bottle of sun
lotion that the sea had brought from Biarritz or some
other French beach, but for me, at the time, it was something precious, and I thought my brother was the best
boy in the world.' That childhood incident, however, was
a long way off, in every sense. Her brother was very different now. He had become a mean, materialistic person,
incapable of imagining a situation in which money did
not play a central role. 'I've been told that you're to have
the workshop in the Old Harbor,' he had said to her very
aggressively on the day when she and Aunt Magdalena
had been making plans for their future. 'Why are you so
upset? And what's so very odd about it, anyway?' she had
retorted. 'You didn't say a word when Father sold you the
shares in the hotel for a nominal price, with the one pro-
viso that you should give me a job in the office. It seemed
fine to you then that you should get everything and that
I should be your employee!' Her brother replied: 'That's
got nothing to do with it. Father had very fixed ideas
about the business. I had no alternative but to accept his
proposal!' Before this discussion ended, she said to him:
'Do you know what we're going to build in place of the
workshop? The best café on the coast!'

Teresa, who led a solitary life and whose sole refuge
was her family, had felt the rift with her brother deeply,
and she pondered the reasons for this transformation,

pondered the secret force which, little by little – with all the determination of something organic, of something that is in the blood and can only manifest itself in silence – had made of her brother an exact copy of their father. She found no answer, but what had happened seemed to her a great misfortune, the second great misfortune of her life. She hated her father with all her heart. 'We're not going to Barcelona now,' she had written in her diary on 2 May 1979. 'My mother and my aunt had everything prepared, but my father came home at midday and said we couldn't go, that this year we had to open the boarding house early and that we could go to Barcelona another time. My mother burst into tears and I got angry and went to spend the night at Aunt Magdalena's house. Fortunately, my aunt took us to the circus. My brother didn't enjoy it very much, but I did. Especially the tightrope walker. His name was Monsieur Gabas and, with only the help of a balancing pole, he walked along a high wire that ran the whole length of the big tent. I thought it was really thrilling.'

Her father was the son of poor fisherfolk, who, having been taken on at the boarding house as a kind of factotum, ended up marrying the owners' eldest daughter and becoming sole manager; he was a man, however, who never lost his servant's heart and who lived with his head permanently bowed before his clientele; yet he was also a man who, like a bad dog, showed no respect for his own family. 'Is that any way to behave towards our friend Signora di Castri? Fancy making such a fuss!' was all he could think of to say when she was sobbing inconsolably and those three words were still echoing in her mind: 'Teresa, *poverina mia!* Teresa, *poverina mia!*' 'So you'd like to come and spend the first two weeks in May here. No problem at all, we'll be expecting you,' he had said to some unknown customer, knowing full well that this would put paid to the trip that her mother and her aunt had been planning for months, knowing too that her mother was ill and that this might be her last chance to travel. And now his son, her brother, behaved in exactly the same way and shared precisely the same values.

After her mother died – in 1981, two years after the ill-fated trip to Barcelona – Teresa had the feeling that she was walking a tightrope, just like Monsieur Gabas whom she had seen at the circus. And yet she had never felt afraid or dizzy or desperate, because her Aunt Magdalena was always there at the other end of the high wire, holding out her hand to her and keeping her from losing her balance. In the bad times, in the really bad times – when there was some problem at the hotel, or when on Sundays and public holidays her single state became more obvious, or when she chanced to hear some malicious remark about her limp that 'woke up the cricket' who would repeat Signora di Castri's words – the mere presence of her aunt made her feel far safer than all the poles in the world. Alas, shortly before Teresa turned 29, on 15 July 1993, the person she loved most in the world, apart from her mother, died.

'This morning we buried Magdalena,' she wrote in her diary on 16 July. 'The church was full of people and many of them came up to me afterwards to say how sorry they were. In a way, it helped me. It was awful weather, very rainy. There was a seagull perched on the mast of a yacht moored in the Old Harbor, and when we passed by with the coffin, it started to scream. Later that afternoon, I shut myself up at home and started cleaning shoes. I must have cleaned at least twenty pairs. Then, for the first time in a long while, I went down to the beach and swam until it was dark. There was a seagull there too. It never left my side, and when I turned on to my back in the water to rest, it seemed to do the same and to hang quietly in the air. It occurred to me then that I was like that bird. Up until now, whenever I've thought about my life, I've always thought of the tightrope walker at the circus, Monsieur Gabas, but perhaps the moment has come for a change of image. The bird hanging in the air more accurately reflects the situation I find myself in.'

Teresa, blinded by the death of the person she had loved, was wrong. She could not be like the bird that had accompanied her as she swam; she could not, as the seagull could, with a simple tilt of its wings, fly up from the waves to the clouds, fly back down from the sky to the rocks or to the roofs of the town. She lacked the strength, the power to triumph over the heaviness of the world, and very soon, she found that she had to make a real effort not to fall into the void. What got her through these times was the monotony of life and the regularity of routine, and she applied herself to this with rigor: from ten until two, she worked in the office at the hotel; between two and three she went to the café in the Old Harbor and had a sandwich, a no. 10, the vegetarian option, at the table reserved for her; until seven o'clock, she stayed at what used to be Aunt Magdalena's apartment, above the café, then returned to the hotel where she worked until nine, spent an hour having supper at the café, ten minutes on the jetty smoking a cigarette, and then went back home, where she would pass what remained of the day watching television or reading a fashion magazine.

When monotony and routine were not enough, when she needed more protection or more diversion, Teresa would go across the border to Biarritz or Bayonne to buy shoes or to have clothes made. For the same reason she had tried to be more sociable and to go to the movies or out to supper with a friend of her brother's who used to phone her occasionally, or to resume, with as much enthusiasm as she could muster, her visits to the beach to swim, something which had always done her so much good. However, she found the latter particularly difficult. The jetty had been built in such a way that getting to the seashore meant trudging across 300 yards of beach, which proved both irritating and painful. Long before she reached the water's edge, her right leg would keep sinking into the soft sand, thus exaggerating her limp. Then the cricket would start to sing again, and Signora di Castri's words would go round and round in her head: Teresa, *poverina mia!* Teresa, *poverina mia!* Teresa, *poverina mia!*

The page she had written on 16 July 1993, the day after Magdalena's death, completed the sixth volume of her diary, and at the time, in the despair of the moment, she decided that she would not write any more, that she would live in silence, without the relief of that private confession. Nevertheless, exactly 40 days later, on 26 August, she bought her seventh notebook and continued writing. The new chapter bore the name of a character who had long been with her: Monsieur Gabas. This was not a reference to the tightrope walker, however, or even to her personal situation.

'Last week, something surprising happened,' began Teresa's entry for that day, a longer entry than usual. 'There was a craft fair on in town, and in the evening, instead of going straight back to the office, I decided to go for a stroll around the Old Harbor where the stalls were set up. After buying a few knickknacks, I was just about to go back to work, when I noticed a stall right at the end of the jetty, one that I hadn't noticed until then; it seemed to be selling wooden toys, and so I went over, thinking that I would just have a quick look. There was a slight breeze, and from the jetty, the sky looked like marble veined with red and green and blue. It was a really lovely evening.

Next to the stall was a man in a white shirt, standing with his back to me and looking out to sea, and, at first, I thought he must be a visitor. But when I started looking at the toys, he turned round and said: "Take your time, there's no hurry." I don't know why, but I felt a kind of shock, as if a bolt of lightning had struck the ground immediately behind me. He was about fifty, with curly, graying hair. He looked rather like the kind of actor who gets cast as Jesus in American movies.

I thought the toys were really lovely, the kind my mother or my aunt would have had when they were children, and I set about choosing one, rather hurriedly, because it was getting late. "If you haven't got time today, come back tomorrow," he said. He had a French accent, I realized then, and this was perhaps why he spoke so slowly, almost sweetly. "Yes, you're right. Your toys deserve more time. I'll come back tomorrow," I said. "About six o'clock?" he said. Again I felt that flash of lightning behind me. The way he said these words didn't sound like a business appointment. I said six o'clock would be fine. Then he held out his hand and introduced himself. His name was André and he was from Bordeaux.

I did the same. I shook his hand and told him my name too.

Our conversation had evolved in such a strange way, as if the jetty in the Old Harbor had provided us with a peculiarly intimate atmosphere, ideal for this quiet exchange, but the most surprising thing of all occurred just as I was leaving. "What name would you give to this doll?" asked André, putting his hand into a box and drawing out... a tightrope walker! It was a doll in the form of a spinning top which, because of its long arms, could remain balanced on a column without falling off. "I'd call it Monsieur Gabas," I replied without a moment's hesitation. "The perfect name," he said, and I had the feeling that there was a thread between us, something binding us together. "I'll expect you tomorrow, then," he said, putting the doll in my purse. I thanked him for the present and walked very slowly and unhurriedly away from the stall.

The following day, as soon as André saw me appear on the jetty, he closed his stall and invited me to go for a walk. "We lame people don't tend to go in much for walking," I said in a steady voice. I felt odd and strangely energized. "What caused it?" he asked. "Infective arthritis?" "Don't tell me you're a doctor as well," I said. "I am actually," he replied coolly. "But I gave it up seven years ago. I used to work in the hospital in Bordeaux." Then he offered me his arm, saying: "If you hold on tight, you won't get tired." I felt slightly giddy, as if I were drunk. "Do you want people to think you're my boyfriend?' I said. He looked into my eyes and smiled broadly. "That's exactly what I do want. I'd like to be your boyfriend. And if you'll allow me, that's what I'll try to become." A few seagulls were flying about above the jetty, very excited about something. I waited for them to fall silent. I felt strong and suddenly very aware that I was from the same stock as Aunt Magdalena. "Why do you want to be my boyfriend, may I ask?" I said. "Because you have the golden eyes of a goat," André replied. Somewhat taken aback by this answer, I insisted: "Is that the only reason?" He smiled again, and looked at me like someone making a calculation. "Well, because of that and because of something Montaigne, the philosopher from Bordeaux, once said," he replied after a silence. "According to Montaigne, a man who has never lain with a lame woman does not know what it is to lie with a woman." He stood still, looking at me hard. For my part, I felt my head becoming considerably hotter than the rest of my body. "I've never heard that before," was all I managed to say. Then I pulled myself together sufficiently to add: "And I've been lame for a long time." In this frame of mind, we walked along the jetty and strolled about for quite a while. We had supper at one of the restaurants with tables on the beach.'

There exists a treatise on love which describes a custom amongst workers in the saltmarshes of Salzburg which involved lowering the branch of a tree down into one of the pits, then taking it out again in summer when it would emerge covered in thousands of salt crystals, glittering in the sun like diamonds, a marvelous phenomenon which the author of the treatise compares with the effects of love on the beloved: 'Just like that branch in Salzburg,' he writes, 'the beloved becomes brilliant, beautiful and full of fine qualities.'

This statement, which may not be applicable to all cases, perfectly described what happened to Teresa: love – a feeling she had always denied herself and which was mentioned only in the pages of her personal diary – entered her heart as it would the heart of a fourteen-year-old, like a whirlwind, sweeping everything before it, and transfiguring the craftsman she had met on the jetty in the Old Harbor. For her, André was the polar opposite of her father and her brother; he seemed to her intelligent, generous, thoughtful, better even than she was, because he was freer, because he lived according to his own values, unconcerned about social position or money. Paradoxically, André's foreignness brought him closer to her, because she too, for different reasons, felt herself to be excluded and obliged to live on the margins of society. Thus this union of extremes came into being: the man who always wore the same sandals and the woman with a hundred pairs of shoes had met on the high wire, in the middle of the void, and had decided to join forces.

'André needs nothing,' she wrote on 5ᵗʰ October. 'He says he had quite enough things when he worked in the hospital in Bordeaux, and that his model now is Diogenes. Apparently, the Emperor Alexander once went to visit Diogenes to tell him that anything he asked for would be given to him. Diogenes' response was to ask him to move out of the way because he was blocking the sun. "So you don't need anything," I say to him sometimes. "Yes, I need a woman with golden eyes like a goat. Oh, and Montaigne, of course," he replies. He's such a wonderful man.'

Generally speaking, when one is happy, one tends to write rather less than when one is unhappy, and Teresa put the seventh volume of her diary away in one of her desk drawers and forgot all about it for nearly two years. On 5 September 1995, the silence was broken. Teresa reopened her notebook and scribbled this:

'André has gone to Bordeaux to teach a course on making toys, and it will be a month before we see each other again. I would go and visit him, but I can't, because my brother is all tied up with sorting out the new golf course, and I've got to take charge of running the hotel. The night before he left, I got angry and was in a foul mood, and he took it badly. My ill temper, he said, struck him as "vulgar." Then he looked very serious and said that ours was a relationship between two free individuals, and that I should have the same respect for the way he lived his life as he had for mine.'

Shortly after André left, Teresa's thoughts grew darker, and her private confessions took on a querulous tone. One day, she wrote about the schoolfriend who had drowned after falling off one of the rocks below the jetty, and how sad that still made her feel; on another day, about her sense of panic at the idea that André might have gone to Bordeaux for good, and how wrong she had been to rest her whole being on one point, just like Monsieur Gabas, 'the doll he gave me on the day we met;' and on another day, about 'how fragile love was,' and how it made her suffer. 'I don't know what stories you're inventing for yourself,' André said during one of their telephone conversations. 'Listen to me, Teresa, stop getting things all out of proportion and just try to enjoy yourself as much as possible. Why don't you go to the beach and go swimming? The waves would wash away all those ghosts filling your head.'

For the first time since her relationship with André had begun, Teresa felt misunderstood. Nevertheless – for she was not the same woman she had been two years before – she decided to resist the tendency 'to weep into her diary' and to follow the advice she had been given:

she would go to the beach, plunge into the water and let herself be buffeted by the waves. But the day on which she decided to do this – 17 September, a Sunday – was not the most opportune of days. There was a strong wind blowing in from the sea, and she found it difficult to walk. It was also very noisy, and there were lots of children playing football and racing around all over the place, and the sand they kicked up inevitably got in her eyes. Worse still, it was low tide. The waves, the succeeding rows of white lines that the waves made with their foam, seemed miles away.

Teresa decided to turn round and go back to the hotel. The wind was blowing harder than ever, and she was afraid it might knock her off balance and throw her to the ground. Then, just as she was thinking this, a ball hit her on the head. She didn't actually fall over, but the noise on the beach vanished and she felt as if she were floating, like a balloon that someone has thrown into the air, having first put a bit of spin on it with their hand. In the air, in the midst of that silence, the cricket stirred its wings and began to sing. The words of Signora di Castri rang out only once, but louder than ever: Teresa, *poverina mia!*

As soon as she reached the hotel, she called Bordeaux, but André, she was told, was teaching and couldn't come to the phone. She hung up and took out her diary.

'Panic,' she wrote at the top of a new page. 'After two whole years, I have just heard those words again. I thought I was cured, that love had worked a miracle. But the cricket is still there inside me. André told me once that if you wanted to get a cricket out of its nest, all you needed was a twig. However…'

Someone was knocking at the door and gently pushing it open, so Teresa broke off her writing. Seconds later, when she had got up from her desk, the door opened fully and she found herself face to face with an old lady. 'Can I help you?' Teresa asked, bemused. The old lady did not reply at once. She began examining Teresa, wide-eyed and open-mouthed. *'Ma che bella!'* she exclaimed at last, taking a step back and opening her arms. *'Ma che bella!'* she said again. These three words were filled with such surprise and admiration that Teresa – finding new, luminous meaning in the compliments and words of praise spoken by Magdalena, André and a few other people, and suddenly fully aware of her situation – burst out laughing, just as, when a jug shatters, the water spills out onto the floor. 'Don't you recognize me, Teresa?' asked the old lady. 'Signora di Castri, it must be years since you were here!' she said, still laughing. *'Ma che bella!'* said the old lady before embracing her. 'But what's that? A cockroach?' she asked, starting back and pointing to an insect that was just crawling in through the door. 'No, it's a cricket, Signora di Castri. It probably lives in the hotel garden,' Teresa told her. It all fitted, everything slotted into place, the ground on which she walked seemed more solid now, with plenty of support along the way.

The phone rang. It was André, concerned about her earlier call. 'I just rang to tell you that I'm really happy and can't wait to see you again,' she said, still looking at Signora di Castri. *'Ma che bella!'* sighed the old lady.

HARKAITZ CANO (Lasarte-Oria, 1975)

As far as I can remember, I spent my childhood in a tree watching the swollen river rush by. Children don't climb trees anymore and the river doesn't rise that high, but those floods and trees appeared in my first book of poetry *Kea behelaino-pean bezala* (1994, *Like Smoke in a Low-Lying Fog*). When I picked the books up at the printer's, I tripped and dropped them all. I thought it was a good sign, as if they had a life of their own.

I am a writer because I have no talent for drawing or music. Those inadequacies, and all my other ones, help me write. You could say that's why my books often have something to do with music, such as *Beluna jazz* (1996, *Dark Jazz*) and *Pasaia blues* (1999, *Pasaia Blues*).

I studied law, but I never worked as a lawyer. I've been doing scriptwriting for a long time. I spent the 1998-99 academic year in New York and ever since then the Brooklyn

Bridge has been part of my spine. The chronicle *Piano gainean gosaltzen* (2000, *Breakfast on the Piano*) was the product of my stay in New York.

My favorite genre is the short story, as witnessed by *Telefono kaiolatua* (1997, *The Caged Telephone*) and *Bizkarrean tatuaturiko mapak* (1998, *The Maps Tattooed on His Back*). Tell a novelist to pack a suitcase and he'll organize an entire move. Not the short story writer. He'll only put in the bare essentials. When a short story unfolds, it fits on the kitchen floor like a map of the city.

My last book was *Norbait dabil sute-eskaileran* (2001, *Someone's on the Fire Escape*).

The Mattress

by

HARKAITZ CANO

Translated by Elizabeth Macklin and Linda White

The roof of the trailer was patched with green asbestos shingles and the dingy interior was filled nearly wall to wall by a large mattress, making it impossible to walk without tripping over it. Sol sat on the edge of the mattress, smoking a cigarette. In addition to serving as a jerry-rigged bed, the mattress was also an office. It had the look of serving in many capacities. The edges were stained with nicotine and coffee, and the mattress was piled with bills, empty beer cans, and instant soup containers. A telephone sat on one corner of the mattress, the dirty mattress. The cord stretched through the window to a telephone pole on the sidewalk where the copper wire was connected to the Telefónica network by a clandestine sailor's knot. The mattress was torn in a thousand places, as if it had been dragged countless times from room to room through doors too small for it. It had been ineptly mended in a dozen places with thread and fishing line of various colors.

A beautiful beach graced the labels of the soup containers scattered on the mattress and the floor. "We're raffling off a trip to the Cayman Islands." The Caymans are Paradise on earth, so they say. Maybe the mattress itself was a map of the world, with its own Cayman

Island, one of those stains, perhaps. Everything that happened in the trailer happened around the mattress. Each blotch had its own meaning, told its own story, just as the names and colors of countries on a map tell us something about the dictator who rules there.

A father and son lived in that trailer of contracting metal, and despite the green asbestos there were leaks here and there in the roof. The door creaked unbearably with the sound of rusty scissors being forced. They lived in a poor neighborhood, at the tail end of a poor neighborhood, and six months ago they had tied the trailer to a tree. And surprisingly, as we saw, they had a clandestine phone. Sol sat on the mattress, smoking his cigarette, and the phone rang.

"Is this Sol?"

"That's me."

"Sol what?"

"Sol, that's all."

"Is that your first name or your last?"

"Both. My father worked in a lighting store. Sol. Sun. Get it?"

"I know I'm asking too many questions. This is Mrs. Garcia. Well, Matusa's my name. Maybe you know me as Lula from number thirteen. Look, it's not easy to say this... I'm sorry to call out of the blue like this and intrude on your family's privacy, but... your son Gabi gave me your number. He's here right now. At our place, I mean. It seems that... well, it's a problem with the kids. Your son stole our son's leather ball, and..."

Leather always meant trouble, thought Sol. The horizon was the color of coffee and cream. The sun was setting. Sol exhaled with a long sigh, blowing an oblong smoke ring.

"I'll be right over."

Number thirteen was the only house in the neighborhood with a painted wall around it. True, it looked shabby, but not as much as the neighborhood's other houses. At first glance it was one of the best-looking and most dignified in the neighborhood, in spite of its smallness. The grass had just been mowed, too. It was dusk, but Sol could still make out three figures at the door of the house. There was Mrs. Garcia, Lula, Matusa, Methuselah, or whatever her name was, a thirty-eight-year-old hysterical female still worth looking at. And there was his son Gabi, head bowed. And the third had to be the boy whose ball Gabi had supposedly stolen, standing there by his mother. He was older than Gabi, Sol figured, thirteen or so, Sol figured. Three years older than his son.

"Do you have anything to say for yourself, Gabi?" His son was silent, staring at the ground as if searching for worms. "You've really embarrassed me in front of people, boy. And it's not the first time. But I swear on my father's ashes, this will be the last. We'll straighten this mess out in a hurry. Now, give the ball back to your friend right now."

"But... I don't have any ball, Dad."

"Liar!" The father yelled, taking his son by the shoulder and shaking him back and forth. "You'd better give the ball back right now, you damn brat, or I'll wring your neck. Forgive me, Mrs. Garcia." He turned to the woman, lowering his voice and softening his manner. "If that ball doesn't turn up, I promise you I'll pay for it myself, and then I'll make the damn brat pay, one way or another. What kind of ball was it?"

"Leather." the other boy spoke for the first time, meekly. With his eyes downcast, his long lashes looked like they could sweep leaves. Sol thought he looked wretched. After a painful silence, he spoke again, hesitantly. "Regulation. It was regulation. New. And leather. It was a special leather ball."

Again, Sol thought, leather brings trouble. He looked at Lula and now saw the hint of a smile in her eyes.

"Okay, ma'am, how much do you think the ball was worth, more or less?"

"We paid over thirty euros for it."

"That much?"

"It was leather, a regulation ball. What's more, it was new."

"Damn. I don't have that kind of money right now, ma'am, but as soon as I get my check on Monday, I'll come right over, I promise. Now, if you'll pardon me, I'd like to have a talk with my son. He's going to regret lying to me!" Sol was furious. He looked as if he really would ring the boy's neck.

He smacked his son on the ear and dragged him out of Mrs. Garcia's yard. Mother and son stood silhouetted against the light, watching them go. Mrs. Garcia put an arm around her son's shoulders. There was no hardness in their eyes now. They looked worried and sympathetic. Maybe Mrs. Garcia regretted her phone call. Those street peddlers had a poor reputation in the neighborhood. She didn't even want to think about the beating that Gabi would get. Matusa lit a cigarette and offered one to her son with trembling fingers. He looked at her in surprise and put the unlit cigarette between his lips. In the end, they'd only done what they had to do. It wasn't just any

ball. There weren't many leather balls in the neighborhood, and even fewer that were regulation.

Reggae music floated from neighborhood windows.
The music eased the tension. All the way back to the
trailer, Sol and Gabi walked in silence, watching the frail
sun sink on the wide horizon. They looked away only
once, a few houses from the trailer, to watch seven-year-
old called Turtle fooling around with a shiny orange bicycle. Gabi may have been thinking of his missing childhood. He was raised on the street, with no toys, always
wandering from place to place, his only homeland the
mattress in the trailer.

When they reached the front door, Sol's ten-year-old
son picked up a rust- and oil-stained cardboard carton
from the junk in the bushes. His father opened the creak-
ing door and they went in, heads bowed. Sol turned on
the light, a wobbling solitary bulb, then lit a couple of
candles, which matched the bitter flame in Sol's eyes.

"Give it here," snapped Sol, holding out his hand.

The father was sitting on the mattress. He moved
instant soup cartons and beer cans to make a place for his
son. Lying next to the phone were half a dozen hits of
speed, a handful of nails, shreds of green asbestos, and
dust that looked like green pollen, and a screwdriver.
God only knew what kind of flea market this was. Gabi
held out the cardboard carton and Sol removed the
leather ball to examine it under the light.

"It's got a hole in it, but it's not bad. With a patch,
it'll be fine. We'll get twenty for sure, maybe thirty with
luck."

His son turned listless eyes on him and smiled wanly
when his father ran a hand through his tar-black hair.

"Okay, now you know where to go next." With a shrug, Sol indicated where.

The corners of the trailer were grimy with candle soot, and the faint light made shadow pictures on the nicotine-stained walls. When Gabi left the unpleasant soupy atmosphere of the trailer and headed for the cold air of the street. It was already pitch dark. When he looked back, he saw a long-legged woman in a short skirt climbing the steps of the trailer. His father ran a finger under the elastic of her panties. Then he squeezed her body against his own and pulled on the elastic until her panties were a thin ribbon, exposing the cheeks of her bottom. It was Friday, and despite what Sol had told Matusa, he hadn't worked that day. It wasn't the first time. Gabi knew that before Monday, maybe Saturday, they would hook up the trailer and leave.

"Okay, now you know where to go next." No more words were needed. Gabi knew his father very well, and he knew what it meant when he saw the sparkle in his father's eyes. He didn't want to leave the neighborhood without taking Turtle's shiny orange bike with them. Chances like this were few and far between. It would be a shame to let this opportunity slip away.

Gabi wondered if Turtle was asleep yet. Hands in his pockets, he headed for Turtle's house. He kicked an instant soup can, and it clattered along for two or three yards. It was one of the cans with the Cayman Islands on the label that said they were raffling a trip to the Caymans, paradise on earth. Luck was on his side. Turtle had left his bicycle in the yard. It was shiny and new and the color of oranges. He leaped over the wall, grabbed the bike, and hurried back toward the trailer. On the way, he stumbled over a beer can on the sidewalk, lost his balance, and fell to the ground, bike and all. The silent calm of the night continued around him, though, and he lay on the sidewalk for a long moment, staring at the can. It was the same brand of beer his father drank. Part of the can was as orange as Turtle's bike, the color of flame, and he asked himself if maybe there wasn't also a hell on earth. He realized he was thinking like a grown man and he didn't much care for it, or for his father, either. Gabi loved him a lot but didn't like him at all. "Dumb-ass digressions" his father would say. And he was digressing, too, although he didn't know what the word meant. It might be trying to catch butterflies in a net with big holes in it or something. Gabi also knew that his father wouldn't let him sleep on the mattress that night, but he longed to be inside the trailer anyway. There, he could peep through one of the holes in the wall and see the hot breath of bare naked flesh as panties fell off a thigh, and he would see the girl's hairy spider eager for his father's tongue, and the fevered movement of naked breasts, and their yowling open mouths, all filtered through green asbestos. He would hunt the images down as if with a net.

He wiped his hands on his torn trousers and lifted the bike to his shoulder. The bike wasn't dented. He had a bleeding left knee, but it didn't hurt too much if he thought about something else. He had to "digress" to keep from feeling the pain.

He wondered if his father had already disconnected the phone line. The last time, he got to untie the sailor's knot himself. Untethering that clandestine phone wire was like leaving port. Gabi thought about the mattress again, the blue mattress that was a map of the world. He had heard somewhere that there were mattresses filled with feathers. But he couldn't even imagine that kind of luxury. The thought of the feathers made him imagine dead birds and crooked beaks inside the mattress, a terrifying nightmare he had once and could never forget. He dreamed he opened the mattress and found the dead birds. As he ran toward the trailer, he hated the city and prayed with all his might that everyone in it would have the same nightmare he'd had.

He hurried along now, careful where he put his feet, and lost himself in the night. He wouldn't sleep much on the floor. The stones beneath his feet seemed soft, as soft as the mattress. He imagined the noise of the springs and the frog sweat of their naked bodies. The last lights on the street went out and he heard the slam of a door.

Then the night closed upon itself, like the edges of a wound.

JAVI CILLERO GOIRIASTUENA (Bilbo, 1961)

My name is Javi Cillero. That will not tell you much, so I'd better add some detail. I studied journalism and translation at university in the Basque Country, and have a Ph.D. in Basque Literature from the University of Nevada, Reno. Detective fiction is my speciality, or perhaps I should say my guilty pleasure?

I have translated works by Mark Twain, Roald Dahl, Charles Dickens, Robert Bloch, Ross McDonald, Ernest Hemingway and F. Scott Fitzgerald into Basque. I have also written a couple of books for children: *Eddy Merckxen gurpila* (1994, *Following Eddy Merckx*) and *Thailandiako noodle izu-garriak* (2001, *The Incredible Swarming Noodles*). And I managed to publish a collection of short stories (*Hollywood eta biok* (1999, *Hollywood and Me*)) before the end of the millennium. Just in case.

In my writing I like playing with parallel action, flash-backs and different points of view. In case you hadn't noticed, I really love cinema, it's just that literature is cheaper to pro-duce. I believe in the therapeutic power of storytelling, and that we all have a story to tell. I go about my writing like a Zen painter: for years I hold my brush in front of a white can-vas, until one day the long-awaited story announces itself and I try to capture it in a few rapid strokes.

O.K. I'm not there yet, but in the course of my journey I have collected a number of stories. Let's put it this way: life is disguised in literature, yet literature reveals life under its own disguise. Now it is time to read on.

A Kiss in the Dark

by

JAVI CILLERO

Translated by Amaia Gabantxo

In the heat of the night you turn towards me under the sheets, my love. You ask me to tell you a story, for you can't fall asleep. Between kisses I look closely into your near-sighted eyes, and clear my throat. You've told me before that I have a baby face, that that's why so many women give me loving looks. That it makes you jealous. If only you knew… the most loving look anyone has ever given me – apart from yours of course, my darling – came from an old woman. This is something that happened a long time ago, something I never told anyone, perhaps because I don't feel comfortable talking about it.

I was fourteen, had just started secondary school, and I had gone into a police station to fill in the forms to request an ID card. They took our picture in a photo shop in Uribarri, and neither of us was overwhelmingly happy as we left the studio, four black-and-white faces on a square bit of paper in our hands. I looked like a child in the pictures, even if the hair I'd grown long gave me an edgier look. As you can see, even back then I had a baby face.

We had to go all the way down one hell of a steep road and cross the entire city to hand over the official photographic documentation for our ID papers. We had to go to Indautxu, on the other side of Bilbao, and even if the mere mention of the word 'police station' made us feel uneasy we had no option but to go. At least it was a good excuse for two young boys to go for an adventurous wander around the city... We seldom went to the center, just to the *Olimpia* cinema or to the arcade in Euskalduna Street, so the city seemed quite labyrinthine to kids from our neighborhood.

As we were crossing the Town Hall Bridge, my friend realized he'd left his money at home. You know, the money you need to pay for the forms and so on. I told him he could borrow some of mine, but when we counted what we had we realized there wasn't enough for the both of us, so he decided to go back home to get some. Then we said goodbye and agreed to meet at the police station.

As I said, I seldom went into the city by myself, and even less often around the Indautxu area. So this was the perfect occasion to indulge in a thorough exploration of the place: the cinemas, the arcades, the shops where you could exchange comics, all the plush bars; I even spotted a dubious-looking 'club' with a red front door as I strolled, going deeper and deeper into the city. The thing was, by the time I'd investigated the whole neighborhood, the doors of the police station were closed. They had very restricted working hours and I would to have to return the next day.

So I thought it was pointless to wait for my friend, and decided to head back home taking an alternative route. Walking this way and that I found myself in an unfamiliar street near the Alhondiga. I looked around me and saw menacing faces staring from street corners. I also saw old warehouses, dusty, broken blinds, dark bars and noisy garages. The heady smell emanating from the garages was making me dizzy, until I panicked and started to run.

I stopped by the traffic lights at the end of the street to get my breath. Suddenly, a wrinkled hand touched my arm. It was a woman, a very old one. She was asking for help in the middle of a busy street in the city center. Why? Because she needed to change a light bulb in her living room, in the ceiling. She was carrying the little globe of glass in her hand, in an attempt to lend veracity to her story. I was sure she had noticed my baby face, and that that was why she was asking me for help. I was totally astonished, my love, but I wasn't able to say no.

Escaping from the boisterous street she guided me towards an old apartment house. The entry was dark as hell, and the wooden staircase looked like it was about to crumble. Inside her flat it wasn't much better, even if a welcoming *Ongi-etorri* sign by the door lent the atmosphere a bit more cheer. The structure of the house was crooked, as shown by several loose planks of wood along the hallway. Someone had taken down the paintings on the walls and in their stead square yellowing stains decorated the corridor. A leaning tower of dirty dishes was piled up in the sink, as if the woman's natural daily rhythm had somehow slowed down in her old age. The sound of a radio filtered into the flat from the patio window, together with the pervasive smell of cabbage.

At last we entered the room in darkness. I was too afraid to climb the decrepit step ladder, so I used a chair instead. When the light flickered and filled the room, I saw collapsed piles of newspapers by the walls. The woman thanked me, and promised to pray to all the saints in heaven for the well-being of my soul. Then she offered me coffee. I was too nervous not to accept, even if the paltry job I'd done hardly deserved payment. In any case, I didn't dissuade her and nodded to express my acceptance. Now I know why. It was that I'd somehow come to understand that her life was being extinguished just as the light in her room, that this was her last bit of light.

She had mentioned coffee, but she had laid out the table elegantly, as if in preparation for a festive meal. She took out two plates and placed the silverware carefully around the table while I looked on in amazement. She seemed at ease as she brought porcelain crockery to the table; I said to myself that she'd done something like this before. Without further ado, she told me to sit down and proceeded to serve the meal so gracefully that she looked twenty years younger.

The woman confessed it was her son's birthday, and that she wanted to celebrate it with me. At that moment she gave me a look of pure love, and if ever I have felt anything like that, it was then. The sort of look, you know, that told me that no matter what I did I'd always be forgiven. Only children are looked at in that way, without a hint of criticism, before the ups and downs of life change all that. By the way, it goes without saying that I don't expect you to ever look at me like that...

We both enjoyed the meal, she with the ladle in her hand, and I with the spoon in my mouth – every dish was a greater delight to the palate. Every now and then she would half-close her eyes and ask after my studies. I told her all sorts of things: how I'd just started in the new school and how I'd failed the math exam. How I spent most of the time drawing, and reading novels, especially during the philosophy lectures. She also told me a few things. How her son lived abroad and she was all by herself. How she never left the house and how even her shopping was brought home to her by a boy from a neighboring grocery shop.

After the meal she turned on the radio and brought me some rice pudding and coffee. I started to worry that the people at home would begin to wonder where I was. Even so, I felt so comfortable sitting on the violet armchair, looking into that woman's pale eyes; I was in great company. That's how I found myself going through her photo album; she'd brought it along with a bunch of letters.

They were old family pictures, in black and white, and the woman was in all of them, younger then, and with a child standing next to her. The pictures had been taken in many places, at times when they'd taken the child out for the day; they were the broken pieces of a past. At the beach in Neguri, under the arches of the Artxanda tramway, in the Plaza Barria, next to the fishing boats by the Areatza quay. Noticing that the woman's pupils dilated quite a bit when she looked at her son, I asked her to tell me some stories about him.

Of course he wasn't a boy anymore, but for her he would always remain so. As a matter of fact, he now worked abroad; he'd started as a ship doctor and eventually found a job in a prestigious clinic in New York. The mother was very proud of her son, and she always kept a place ready for him in that old house of hers, with a bed ready-made, waiting for the boy to arrive. Unfortunately he hadn't come back to Bilbao for a very long time. That was why he sent her post cards and photographs.

Then she took out her favorite picture of her son: it showed a mustached young man wearing a linen suit, with a big nose and sad eyes and a weak smile on his lips. He looked like Rock Hudson. The young man was smoking. He needed the cigarette in order to look sophisticated, and I committed that observation to memory. I told her that he looked like a really nice guy; that he looked like her, especially around the eyes and nose. I don't know why, but I felt embarrassed, and guilty, as if I might stain her son's picture.

In the end I had to tell her that I needed to leave, because she was ready to show me all sorts of other mementoes. She wouldn't let me go until she'd pressed a hundred-peseta note into my hand. In the hall by the staircase, in the dark, she planted a kiss on each of my cheeks, and without adding anything else, told me to be good and work hard. Once again she looked at me with incredible tenderness.

It had started to rain lightly, and I hurried all the way back to my neighborhood. Back then it always used to rain like that in Bilbao, my love, a thin, weightless rain. That's why I was rushing back home, and getting lost more than once. Clearly, I hadn't memorized my way out of the labyrinth.

I won't tell you how I hid the money, or about the screaming session that awaited me at home. But I'm sure you'd like to know whether I ever saw that woman's face again.

Not right away, at least, no.

I was forced to go and sort out my ID papers again. Even so, I went there with my friend and didn't have a chance to return to the woman's neighborhood. Besides, I couldn't exactly remember which street she lived in, and since she never went out, there wasn't much I could do...

After a month I'd forgotten the whole adventure. And then spring came.

In the spring my nose would be totally blocked and I'd be unable to breathe. After wasting a dozen boxes of vaccinations, they took me to the family doctor. The doctor sent me to the Deusto infirmary to get my polyps removed. I'd be in and out in a few hours.

Mother and I walked all the way to the nose-and-throat doctor's surgery.

I remember the floor and walls were covered in tiles, just that. That and the doctor's redolent, reverberating surname, which I shall never forget. After sitting poor me down on a chair, the doctor laid out the surgical instruments he needed for the intervention. He gave me a local anesthetic, grabbed a gimlet and sat down in front of me. The lamp he was wearing on his forehead didn't let me see him, and I had to hold tight onto my chair when he inserted the pincers in my nostrils.

A little while later I noticed a burning smell and then a little smoke, nothing else. When he'd finished, the doctor removed the lamp from his forehead, and stayed there, staring at me with a smile, satisfied with his work. Bit by bit the features around that smile became clearer, and I saw a big nose and sad eyes, and a thin moustache.

And then, the doctor lit a cigarette.

JUAN GARZIA GARMENDIA (Legazpi, 1955)

A dishful for this fool (my life and works)

The chief date of my life is the day – the night (February 7, 1955) – just before I was born. That evening, my mother-to-be's last dinner (about 22:30 is a normal Basque dinnertime) was at least a half kg of good black-backed elvers (the prices weren't what they are today). This might explain – but not justify, of course – a lot of things about my personality: these question-like curls and spiraling breaks in syntax and behavior, that sybaritic gluttony of the unknown... and other kinds of oddity better known to Mr. Freud (in fact, it was the bait of that dish of elvers that lured me into this world). It was a rather busy digestion that night, both my mother's and mine, and I keep on doing it even now, though by other means (i.e. secreting metaphorical ink-sweat, progressively blackening my elver-self as it grows into an adult eel, having epically swum from the remote sea to reach its mother's creek, and then, if not yet caught, soon parting again from the sweet waters towards the deadly ocean of its birth...). It has perhaps been worth it, even if just to tell the story again. From that particular night on, my biography is trivial. The rest – what is left out, and what may somehow slow wild living – is not yet perfect silence, but some imperfect (short, too short) stories and a number of translations that could paint, all together, the illusory portrait of one of my selves. But these are too many little selves from only a half kg of elvers.

[Editor's note: J. Garzia has published a novel, *Fadoa Coimbran* (1995, *The Fado in Coimbra*), a book for children, *Sudur puntan mundua* (1994, *The World at the End of Your Nose*), and two collections of short stories, *Akaso* (1987, *Perchance*), and *Itzalen itzal* (1993, *Shadow of Shadows*).]

Gubbio

by

JUAN GARZIA GARMENDIA

Translated by Kristin Addis

AN UNKNOWN MEDIEVAL WOMAN POET

Virginia Ossiani, reporting from Gubbio

Gubbio is gray. Its rooftops are gray, the walls of its houses are gray, gray are the paving stones of its streets. This gray is not slate however. Gubbio was built of stronger and nobler stones; even the *Palazzo dei Consoli* is made of the same stone, a rigid mass there upon the gray hill, in the center of the medieval part of town, casting its shadow from one side of the square plaza that looks out over the village.

The visitor who comes to Gubbio will see this from below: a gray-stoned medieval village going straight up from left to right on a small hill, the enormous silhouette of the Palazzo the balancing point for the rows of houses.

Our traveler doesn't know what he will find here. In fact, Gubbio's only fame is as the town where Saint Francis famously spoke with the wolf, and the traveler arrives from Assisi having already had his fill of tourist hoopla centering around the saint. Perhaps because of this, he appreciates the medieval authenticity of the gray houses clustered together, the uniform roughness of the crude stones. As he walks along looking around, still at the foot of the town, he runs into the lively crowd at the market. A peasant atmosphere: sellers' intermittent clamor, the awnings gleaming under the full sun.

After a while, he goes on up through the shadowy streets, gazing idly at the iron trimming at the entrances of both the elegant stone-hewn houses and the less dignified ones. The shine of black iron against the gray matte of stone.

Ornaments, tools, arms… Steel has always been worked in Gubbio. The citizens' hands and faces are gray with iron dust, their eyes saddened from contemplating molten iron.

Our visitor doesn't know the news – he doesn't read the local newspapers – of the discovery that honors the region these days. Yet it seems the local people have long ago lost the capacity to be surprised by anything. Ever since the terrifying wolf was tamed by the *Poverello* and went from house to house meek as a puppy until it died of old age, it seems they have mined the last of their wonder. Or perhaps they simply haven't heard the news.

The whole thing started when they began renovations on the chaplain's house. The building is beautiful in fact, but old, and the long abandonment and poor location, unprotected from wind and rain, have left it completely destroyed. They want to turn it into a cultural center. It was when they were carrying out these renovations that the old manuscript which is now causing such a hubbub first came to light. The pages were concealed in a hiding place in the very stones, and that explains to some extent not only why they were still there, but also why the parchment has held up so well.

There's little doubt about the author except for his name: the manuscript was written by a priest, a chaplain of the Order of Saint Clare, the main text in the Umbrian dialect with some passages in Latin. The date is estimated to be the middle of the thirteenth century. There are thirty-three pages and, though one might cast doubt on the more unbelievable aspects of the story they tell, or on the chaplain's intentions for these pages, there is fundamentally nothing to disbelieve in the basic information they give us. Whether they were for the Inquisition or were kept under the secrecy of the confessional, whether the confused fantasies are the reporter's own or the priest's pen augmented them, these are trivial matters; in our opinion, the tribulations of the protagonist are the candid mirror of a true event. If this is so, the documents found now by chance tell us of another unfortunately unrecoverable work, as well as of an unknown poet's name and movements.

So as not to break the thread of our story's dramatic course, I will stick to the chaplain's version, leaving to the perception of the reader the task of separating the wheat from the chaff to determine the truth of the matter, though I will try to keep my version as short and free of digressions as possible since our goal is not to produce a literary recreation of the chaplain's text, but to present the news of this lost literary trail to the readers of this newspaper; that is, to make the inevitably circuitous introduction of Bettina Mariani, forgotten poet nun.

Before we start, let us state that the chaplain received all these details from Bettina's friend and confidante. Bettina told her afflictions to only one other person, another nun slightly older than herself with whom she had this special relationship. The confidante was a gawky woman, skilled in the garden and in the kitchen. Her name was Dorotea Viglione, and it is thus to her that we owe this important testimony, though (as we will see later) she was rather simple by nature and – as naiveté is wont to be – with a penchant for embroidering her vision of reality with her own personal ghosts. This simplicity would have made her, perhaps, more beloved in Bettina's eyes. Nevertheless, it is hard to know how much of the story has come down to us from Bettina and how much from Dorotea; and of course we must not forget that the chaplain would also have made his own contribution when completing the story.

Bettina Mariani was a nun in the convent founded in Gubbio by Saint Clare on the orders of Saint Francis. From the time she was very young, she was disposed to poetry. She was consumed by a sentimental passion for God, and He gave her the inspiration to sing His cosmic joy in the humblest things. It is not surprising, therefore, that she soon entered the Second Order of Saint Francis. She was dearly loved by the other nuns, who marveled at her gift for verse, both when it took flight toward the mystical, and when it humbled itself in songs for common celebrations.

God, Poetry... these are big words. Bettina loved nature. She gathered all her feelings in it, it was the basis for all her mysticism, and to it she dedicated all of the time left free to her by her chores and prayers. Roaming alone in the mountains was her most deeply felt devotion, and these walks gave her, apart from the satisfaction of her soul, breathing space for her poetry as well. With time, the rumor of the poet nun Bettina spread to other convents, together with the most serviceable pieces of her work: songs, readings for prayers... Outside the convents as well, it was told that there was a poet nun among the Poor Clares of Gubbio.

Bettina had found her favorite spot on a mountain slope where she went on the most beautiful days to lie down on the grass to imagine the face of God in the greatness of the farthest mountains and in the limitless blue of the heavens.

At times like these, she would take along her writing tools; since she felt such a deep communion in that place, she loved to write down right there the divine poetic sparks that came to her suddenly. She wanted her pen dipped in the experience of nature that entered all her senses.

Thus it was with joy she saw what a gorgeous day it was that late winter day. She had fewer opportunities that late in the season, and she spent the whole day waiting anxiously for the time when her duties would leave her free to go to her favorite place.

She set off then finally, our nun, in the late afternoon, up the craggy path between the hawthorns, longing to taste of her small paradise in the beauty of that beautiful day.

The sunset was as miraculous as only a March afternoon can provide. If she intended to return before darkness, it was already time to take the road back, but suddenly she came to her senses as if waking from a dream, speechless, stunned, in a trance: God Himself had been given to her in her contemplation, and she was capable of putting Him into words. But then she realized she had forgotten her writing tools, her need to get out into the mountains had been so compelling that day.

At the same time, she noticed that it was getting late; the darkness was forcing the light to retreat from the mountain peaks, even as the divine glow of those heavenly words was already darkening in her forgetful earthly memory. And she felt fear in her bowels.

If she went along the path repeating the words, maybe she could fix them in her consciousness, but it frightened her that if a single word twisted on her, God's living presence would leave her and there would be no way to get it back, not even if she spent her whole life in that place. Without completely realizing what she was doing, she picked up a stick from the ground, from the side of a holly tree speckled with red and, where there was an empty space on the ground beneath the tree, started to write there with the stick. She scored the words in deeply; the ground was soft and she started to calm down. In this also, she thought she had found a message from God: these words were to be written without elaborate tools; what nature had given was to be returned to nature by nature.

When she had finished the poem, night was upon her and she got back on the road to the convent; not, however, without looking back often along the path. She was already longing for the approaching night to give way to the light of the new day. She sped back to the convent.

There to endure the long night. In the convent her songs for the festival of Saint Joseph danced in the air, but Bettina's mind was on the coming dawn. She retired early not because she was sleepy, but to be alone. And she waited, without the comfort of sleep.

She opened her window to the first ray of light. Her eyes were blinded by the white glare of the snowfall; the ground was completely obscured. Seized by a sweeping panic, she ran to the holly tree, her rustic ash-gray habit trailing through the snow. Throwing herself to her knees, she began to claw away the snow. The snow was so deep it reached halfway up the holly tree. When finally she cleared it away, there was a muddy mess in the place where Bettina had hoped to find her mystic cry, the incomparable words that gathered the silence around them. She did not give in to tears, but a thin wail arose from deep inside her and expanded, seeking its echo, a lament held on a single note and cutting a deep wound in that vast white stillness.

From then on she seemed dead to life. Whenever her duties at the convent allowed her, she would return to the side of her holly tree to weep over her lost poem. And she fell totally silent.

The convent's vow of fasting was rigid, but Bettina took it even further. As though she intended to keep her mouth shut in this as well, she gave up joining the others in the dining room in case mealtimes would force her out of her silent solitude. Rather than eat or sleep, she spent these hours before a white parchment in the isolation of her room, giving body and soul to the attempt to rescue the brilliant rays of those words from the black pool of forgetfulness. She became terribly thin. The failure of memory, instead of making her despair, only left her mad with stubbornness: her only appetite was to complete that text again. As the days passed, she became but a pallid bag of bones.

Dorotea was hurt when Bettina wouldn't talk to her either: what could she do to console her friend? Her pain became unbearable when she recognized that Bettina's health was deteriorating ever more. And, seeing that Bettina was starting to look like a white shadow, it seemed to Dorotea that she must soon depart this world for sheer lack of weight, and she broke confidence to tell the Mother Superior what was happening to her friend.

The Mother Superior owed her decision more to Bettina's silence than to her own good judgment, since she saw no clear way of dealing with this situation. Since even the prayers that she said in solitude didn't bring her the clarity of the heavens, she followed the advice of Saint Clare for such impossible cases and decided to send Bettina to Assisi, to the Saint.

And so Bettina set off with the measured gait of a pilgrim who doesn't want to air his grief, head bowed in humility until she was lost from sight, and guarding the same fixed muteness that might have been seen as pride in the eyes of those left behind at the convent, now cast as sincere obedience. She had left a cloud of envy behind her; they all would have liked to go. They had made her wear a new habit, humble, yet elegant enough in its unpatched grayness that she would not be judged too eager in her show of poverty.

Her habit got muddy and torn on her journey of so many leagues. Brambles and filth, suffering and exhaustion – Bettina nevertheless felt restored by the time Assisi came into sight at the foot of the mountain. She had been infused with a ray of hope fed by the beneficial silent tedium of the journey: if anyone could, the saint would be able to remedy her pain.

She made her entrance into the *Porciuncula* with a need to believe in what is known as the last chance, wanting to cheat the cracks of despair with frantic gestures of faith. She couldn't hide her uncertainty. Her face gave her away. "What ails you, sister?" the poor saint asked her as soon as he set eyes on her. As if this one question had unclothed her mind, Bettina's eyes unexpectedly widened and she turned them to the ground in shame. She had to turn her thoughts to the coarse feel of her habit to make herself believe she wasn't naked, but she achieved just the opposite effect: her mind was_lured to the thought that the pale clothing of the slender man gently smiling at her was even now stroking his naked skin. But when she found the strength to speak, she didn't hesitate: she spilled out her anguish to him as if to someone who already knew everything.

After a short silence, Saint Francis said to her, "My beloved little sister, why does it matter to you that the most exalted should write in human letters? God gave you this gift, and God chose not to leave you a trace of it. Do you not see the ray of His light in all things both inanimate and living, in even the smallest and most humble? And isn't it enough for you that for that moment you were the receptacle of a new revelation, that God in His goodness chose you, from among all the humble creatures of this world, to bear His Word and offer it to the earth? Could there be anything more pleasing outside of heaven? Truly He has made you an equal of the Virgin Mother herself, sister, and yet you complain, ungrateful thing that you are. What insane pride has you in its grasp? You should recite Mary's song of joy in wonder: *God made me to bring marvel to the world, I who am unworthy…*

Bettina fell to her knees then at the feet of the saint and hid her head in his rumpled robes, grasping them with crooked hands.

"Be humble, sister, and meek, but do not despair, for the Father has filled you with His Spirit, even as He blessed me with the Stigmata. Here: kiss these wounds, for benevolent Jesus has paved the path to heaven for us with his suffering on the cross. Have faith only in Him, and see God's greatness in your humility, the glory of heaven in the nothingness of the world, if you would that one day your singing soul would nest with Him forever."

Kissing the saint's pierced hands, Bettina gazed up at him, her hands in his, weeping.

"And now return to your sisters in the peace of God; in the name of the Father and the Son…"

But on the road home, Bettina found no such peace. The blossoming hope that had sprouted in the silence of her journey had wilted with the words of the saint. She had not gone seeking consolation, but asking for a miracle. The saint had not realized this however, and she had not dared to try to turn his actions to her will. Solace… What solace had he offered her other than despair itself? She wants to recover her lost poem, and that's all she wants. He who was able to speak with a wolf, how could he not be able to understand a woman? Or is he perhaps not such a powerful miracle worker as he's famed to be, and therefore was deaf to her petition?

Feet to the trail, mind brooding, a dark thought sprouts from her silent spirit and like a deranged plant takes root and grows, step by step, league by league, the wild expansion of the plant's foliage closing off the light of the sun to the point of extinguishing it. Soon, choked in the black underbrush, her belief in Francis' sainthood wilts: is his pride not greater than hers, forcing her to see the symbols of Jesus Christ's martyrdom repeated in himself? In fact, Francis' life is nothing but a poor imitation of Christ's. He dares to compare himself with Him? And she, may she not hope and desire that God will keep His gift alive in her? The Virgin Mother, he said – what was the Virgin Mother then but a woman, Mary, chosen to be the mother of His Son... though a virgin without original sin, she was untouched but by the Spirit when God the Father chose to make a fleshly son; a non-man, an unclean flow of blood, like all of Eve's lineage. A receptacle, he said. Exactly, nothing but a vessel to be filled by someone else... what was Saint Clare herself then if not the Beloved Sister of Saint Francis? The mother of a son, the sister of a brother, the wife of a husband, all women always something in relation to a man. God's Mother Mary, Saint Francis' Sister Clare, one of Jesus' wives Bettina... Always someone's. Always someone's what? Even with Christ himself as son, brother, husband. Was this perchance woman's worldly existence, as angels serve in heaven? Since a woman cannot celebrate mass, is it then impossible that she might write the poem of poems, know God more intimately than the saintliest of men, as deeply as the angels...? Angels. Angels also have men's names: Gabriel, Raphael... The fallen as well as the heavenly: Lucifer... And God himself, who said he had to be a man? Does God not appear in mystic ecstasy as neither man nor woman, nor yet even human? In the name of the Father and the Son... he had dismissed her. The Holy Spirit must also be male of course, in its image as a dove, right, brother Francis? The Holy Trinity: the begetting dove, the mighty father, and the fruit of the womb. There had to be a womb: Mary. Return to your sisters, he said, he who was said to turn wild beasts into angels; bow before me and go, little sister, tiny Virgin, return to the humble work of God's wives, you are nothing yourself.

She entered Gubbio with the darkness. A distant wolf howling at the yellow moon rising over the convent. By now winter has drawn back to the mountain tops.

Dorotea was shocked at the countenance Bettina presented to her that night, and even more at the scandalous ideas that she spoke in a distant monotone. It seemed Bettina was speaking to herself rather than to her. And she wouldn't be able to keep her friend's chilling secrets if Bettina remained long in this state of non-being. But one week later – apparently done some good by her long walks in the mountains – she had changed completely, a change for the better if not a return to her earlier self. Dorotea was very happy. Also very relieved: what Bettina had said before in anger and all the senseless heresy in words she didn't really believe was, of course, nothing but overexcitement, like when children become obstinate. Dorotea had nothing to worry about any more; she would keep praying, however, for God to pardon Bettina's scandalous words and make her forget about them.

With the spring, an enchanting smile blossomed on Bettina's face. In the summer, to the delight of the whole community, her body slowly returned to health, and her face grew beautiful. By fall, she had the look of a Madonna.

And thus winter arrived, and with it, Christmas.

Just before dinner on Christmas Eve, the nuns were gathered around a cozy fire, chatty and songful, red-cheeked. But suddenly, where's Bettina? and a worry ignites around the fire, spreading quickly in sparkles of anxious looks, nervous flames that nearly singe the cheeks. Then, as if impelled by a common burning heart-beat, the flock of nuns splits up to search the whole building. No trace of her anywhere however, and they gather again to debate what to do, like swallows returning to roost after having flown. The snow is piling up outside.

It would be insane conceit to even try to go outside, and completely useless to try to go out searching in the closing darkness in which even the snowflakes look black; before anyone suggests this ill-advised plan, the Mother Superior, having hushed the nuns' murmuring, forbids them to so much as mention any such thing.

Dinner remains on the table, witness to the evening's happiness lost in vain. They decide to spend the whole night in prayer. The unchanging clamor of the prayers and the intermittent crackle of the fire's sparks wind around the silence of the evening. Long and anxious, little by little the hours die out with the fire.

The prayers are over. Beneath the pot hook in the fireplace the ashes lie quiet. Day breaks on the dawn of the Nativity. Now the nuns proceed clumsily in the soft snow, some in twos or threes, some in larger groups, some alone, spreading out aimlessly in dwindling hope in this endeavor. Or perhaps we should say flight. One alone among them goes to a known destination, led by another kind of instinct: Dorotea, shovel in hand, falling down and getting up stubbornly on the mountain path erased by the snow.

And there, in the place where Bettina's mystic poem turned to soil, Dorotea found her, dead in the snow by the holly tree, just as she had feared.

There ends the part that interests us, the part that tells us about Bettina Mariani's life, that is. But let us explain, nonetheless, in case anyone is curious, how poor Dorotea describes her search for the body in the chaplain's version of the story.

Dorotea on the path to Bettina's favorite place, breathing hard, eyes wide, is blinded to the high snowy plain by the fierce sunlight. Mountain solitude, resplendent and white. By the holly tree, however, something or someone is scratching at the snow. A red-haired beast, apparently a newborn wolf cub. When she approaches it, it turns to her and stares and it has the face of a child, a head of golden curls, like in images of Baby Jesus!

Dorotea thinks she will faint, unable to hold the sacrilegious gaze of this impossible beast in the sharp white snow-sun. And then she notices its umbilical cord, just there, still dangling, losing itself in the deep snow. Something she doesn't want to believe in gives her the strength from somewhere to kneel there and begin to dig, following the dark cord in the snow under the heartrending stare of the small scratching beast. And there, inescapably, from beneath the gray habit darkened by wetness, the umbilical cord. In the packed down snow, a pool of blood. In her frozen whiteness, Bettina's face shows the beatific sweetness that comes at the last to those who freeze to death. She looks like an alabaster virgin.

Dorotea has long since reached the depths of fear. On top of all the anxiety and confusion, an idea has overcome her, a clear thought that darkens other thoughts: nobody has to know about this. She follows the trail of the umbilical cord with her eyes, determined to kill the newborn monster right there. Then the beast-child stops scratching and looks at her. Dorotea raises her shovel and cuts the umbilical cord so it can leave that place: who would have the heart to harm this creature? But the monster moves toward its mother and starts to lap at the bloody slushy snow with its tame small-god face.

Dorotea, blind with the unbearability of this tableau, hits it and smashes its head without stopping, again and again beating it with the shovel, ripping it apart with a savage passion until she leaves a bloody mess of the beast's intolerable child's face, melting into the reddened slush it was licking at in the snow.

Having finally returned to her senses somewhat she thinks, in the utter exhaustion of that blindness, she lets the bloodied shovel fall from her hands and when she looks with stunned eyes, she thinks she sees in the reddened snow a series of letters taking form in an unbelievable calligraphy, melting under the sun.

She took Bettina's body back to Gubbio, dragging it through the snow. The nuns, having given themselves over to weeping, asked for no details. A corpse has a quieting effect; it's the missing who inspire unease. That night not even the howling of wolves awakened the nuns from their restful sleep after weeping; the bearer of the body was awakened however, lacking the friendly comfort of tears in the night. The next day they buried Bettina, singing the songs she had written. Dorotea had no disposition for such things; a wail would be the only sound that could escape her, so she sat without opening her mouth, wide eyes blurred by the tearful music.

Some passages, without doubt, must be reported as hearsay, but we prefer to present them as our predecessors did, so that the telling might maintain some kind of unity. In the chaplain's text it is clear that the incidents are reported exclusively from Dorotea's perspective. For her at least, that's how things were, and in this sense, they are completely true. On the other hand, were it not for the burden on poor Dorotea's conscience, we would surely have ended up without the story and, as a result, the evidence of the poet nun of Gubbio, like that of so many others, would have been lost forever. In fact, though Dorotea kept it secret her whole life, she wanted to leave this world for the next having made her peace, and thus, before death, she had the chaplain receive her confession, the story that marked her life through her own unsought prominence. May the three of them enjoy the peace they deserve, in the lap of the One who is said to have been made manifest in the lost poem of Bettina Mariani.

ARANTXA ITURBE (Alegia, 1964)

My name is Arantxa Iturbe. Before I knew what I wanted to be in my life, I knew what I wanted to do: I wanted to write. And with that aim in mind I did Media Studies at university, believing that that path would help me realize my dream of earning a living from writing. But on the way, I was seduced by radio. I wanted to tell stories rather than write them, and that's what I have been doing for years: telling stories into a microphone on a radio program.

Out of the blue, one day at the radio station a friend tempted me: "So, how about writing something?" I wrote every day, to tell stories, but not to leave the stories in written form. And from that day on I started writing, and still do.

Mostly, I write short stories. Perhaps because in them, I can combine my job with my passion. Maybe because when I tell a story I like it to be precise, quick, direct and short.

I have published a couple of short story collections: *Ezer baino lehen* (1992, *Before Anything Else*) and *Lehenago zen berandu* (1995, *It Was Late Before*) and a bitter chronicle of motherhood: *Ai, Ama!* (1999, *Oh Mom!*). And I haven't lost my taste for telling stories to those who are too lazy to read. It's finding the time that's difficult. Coming across it.

I tell stories so that someone will listen to them, and write them so someone will read them. But, even so, if I knew that no one listened to what I said or read what I wrote, that wouldn't make me alter my choice: I have hit the bull's eye with my job and my passion. My heart is satisfied. Not something that is easily done.

Maria and Jose

by

ARANTXA ITURBE

Translated by Amaia Gabantxo

Maria's first husband broke her heart, the second broke her teeth, and the third broke her new car.

Jose's first wife stole his heart, and the second all the money in his bank account.

When Maria met Jose, everything she had was in pieces.

When Jose met Maria, he had nothing.

When Jose came to Maria and asked, Maria offered him a place to sleep. For one night.

A month later they were sleeping in the same bed.

They didn't boss each other around.

They didn't talk about the future.

They never mentioned love.

Jose started working as a car mechanic. He would arrive at Maria's house with his hands covered in oil. She would wash them very carefully with a special soap. She didn't want him to stain the sheets.

Once they brought a car to the garage that had been almost totally wrecked in a crash.

"If you can fix it it's yours," said Jose's boss.

And he worked for an extra hour every day until he fixed it. Maria didn't ask him any questions. Jose didn't say anything, even if every night when he returned the dinner on the table was cold.

"Look Maria," screamed Jose as he started the car. Maria was frightened. She had never seen Jose happy.

"I'll take you to see the sea if you want!" he shouted from the street.

And Maria answered yes.

On the way to the sea, Maria thought that living with a man who won't break your things comes close to happiness. When they reached the coastline, Jose began to think that finding a woman who won't steal your things is enough to make you happy.

Without leaving the car, without saying a word, they kissed.

For the first time.

The Red Shawl

by

ARANTXA ITURBE

Translated by Amaia Gabantxo

B ecause she never found anything other than bills and advertising flyers in her post box that pink envelope surprised her enormously. After looking carefully at the front and the back of the envelope (more than once she had got excited about post and then realized it was for one of her neighbors), she noticed it carried no name. Neither name nor address, and that surprised her even more. But she was dumbstruck when, even before reaching the elevator (she was too curious to wait until she got home), she tore the envelope open and read what was inside.

Three words only. In very neat handwriting, well thought out, exactly in the middle of the page: "I love you." No signature, no stamp, nothing. Those three words, next to one another. She read them half a dozen times and thought, at the same time, how seldom she'd heard them. Following that thought through, she decided someone must have put the letter in the wrong post box and went to bed.

She did remember it the day after, but she mostly thought how lucky the intended recipient of the letter was. Until she found a second one in the same post box — her own.

Another pink envelope. And again with no name or address, but this time there was a slightly longer message inside: "For every passing day I love you more."

This second letter wasn't enough. Humans are the only animals that trip over the same stone twice, as the Spanish saying goes, and she went home thinking that the nameless lover had stumbled again. But she didn't stop thinking about it until she fell sleep. 'Why not?' she asked herself. 'Why shouldn't someone fall in love with me?' The thought brought a smile to her face, which intensified the faint lines on it, but she awoke with the first light of day in a very good mood.

Two days later she received the third: 'Don't get nervous. You know who I am. A smile would be enough.' And what if it were true? What if someone, somewhere, was truly taken by her? If he'd at least given her a small clue… She made a mental list of all the men she knew and she couldn't imagine any of them sending anony-mous letters. Joakin, the butcher, liked her, he treated her very well every time she went in to buy ribs, but she couldn't for a minute see him using pink envelopes. Don Ramon, well… the thought of it! She'd been his secretary for twenty-two years now and in all that time he had never directed one sweet word to her – to think that he might start with such nonsense at this stage! Surely it couldn't be him! That would be terrible! Now, that was a silly thought…

And who said it ought to be a man? What if it was a woman? That would make sense. Of course, that was why she didn't dare tell her directly! Just thinking of it sent shivers up her spine, so she decided to drop the sub-ject there and then and go to sleep.

The next one arrived before the end of the week, with this peculiar request: "If you want to know who I am, wear a red shawl across your shoulders." A red shawl! Where would she get a red shawl from? Well, I never, what cheek! It seemed like a crazy thing to do, but she decided that just this once – well, the whole thing was so strange – she'd go up and ask Rosa Mari, her new neighbor.

"I'm really sorry, this is very forward of me, but... would you by any chance have a red shawl I could borrow...? There's this meeting I have to go to tomorrow..."

Rosa Mari was delighted to lend her a shawl. Of course she could have it and no, it was no bother at all, and in fact, did she know what? She was giving it to her as a present, what the hell. She was tired of that shawl... "And if you ever need anything else, feel free to ask away – what else are friends for?"

That night she hardly slept. She spent the night lost in a sea of dreams, waking up with a start from most of them. She couldn't really see herself wearing the red shawl, but the truth was, if that's what it took to meet her mysterious anonymous letter-writer, she would just put it on and go out.

And that's what she did. She selected the clothes that would complement the shawl best and out she went, feeling terribly glamorous. She didn't feel so glamorous on her return. All through the day she looked everywhere. She walked slowly and took detours in every direction, more than ever, on her way to work and back, but no one approached her. By that evening the day that had started so promisingly had quite depressed her.

The day after she opened her post box in a flurry of excitement after noticing the pink envelope from the outside, and read: "Why did you lend your wonderful red shawl to that granny? Should I take this as a definite 'no'?"

ANJEL LERTXUNDI (Orio, 1948)

All writers are in search of something they'll never find. Writers love words, and if ever they do find a fraction of that something, they know that words are the key that brought them there. That is also true in my case. Even though nobody forces me to, I have also been searching, from before the time my first short story collection (*Hunik arrats artean*, 1971) was published, because all writers are writers long before they write their first book (or, at least, readers who dream of being writers). So, I used to read, and that is still mostly what I do, looking for the valuable clues in the stories of those who, like me, have been searching. I also write. But I won't find what I am looking for, because I don't even know what it is, exactly.

Those who approach my work (around ten novels, a couple of essay collections, quite a lot of stories for children and young people, and the following short story collections: *Hunik arrats artean* (1971, *Wait Until Dusk*), *Aise eman zenidan eskua*

(1980, *You Gave Me Your Hand So Easily*), *Urtero da aurten* (1984, *Yearly Means This Year*) and *Piztiaren Izena* (1995, *The Name of the Beast*), will probably notice the zigzagging hesitation that has characterized my search. Furthermore (this is my hope, at least), they'll notice the effort that has gone into that search: the search for a language that speaks freely and calmly. But none of what I've just said is altogether certain.

Berlin Is Not So Far Away

by

ANJEL LERTXUNDI

Translated by Amaia Gabantxo

Sidling up behind me, the museum attendant asks me to change my backpack around and carry it on my stomach. I tell him the security people checked it at the entrance, that there's nothing dangerous inside it.

"The backpack itself is dangerous, sir. What if you were to turn around and damage a painting with it?" He justifies his appeal by pointing at the *Madonna with Child,* by Jean Fouquet, in front of which we are standing.

I find it rather peculiar that Denis should formulate his request in front of the *Madonna* (in my mind the blue-uniformed museum attendant is called Denis: even though it is quite foreign-sounding, to me, at least, the name doesn't seem truly foreign), because it is an interest in this specific painting, and not any other, that brings me to the museum.

I thank Denis.

I turn my attention back to Jean Fouquet's most famous artwork. The rounded shapes of the painting have always made me marvel: the Virgin's naked breast, the left one, which acts as the focal point of the painting and looks like a juicy apple that has just been plucked; her cheeks, which are perfect little circles; the feet, bellies, chests and even heads of the child on her lap and the angels in the background, which have no harsh edges, but are totally round…

I have the entire afternoon to enjoy the painting, which until then I have only admired in reproductions. And through my observation I shall attempt to unearth the very many secrets those lines and curved profiles have almost hidden from me; this will be my pleasure.

One of them is what I shall call the dissension of the eyes: the Madonna, the child and nine angels appear in the painting; all in all, eleven pairs of eyes. But they gaze in different directions, and that is bewildering: logic dictates that the angels and the Madonna should be looking at the child. But no. The angels' looks are scattered everywhere, as if they were birds flying from a tree someone had thrown a stone at. As befits a Madonna, her gaze is directed downward, but, surprisingly, her eyes do not rest on her child, but on her naked breast (a curious fact, one that contradicts what is customarily expected of a Madonna, or a mother). And what about the child's gaze? Why is he the only one looking beyond the painting? What is there to the right of him (the left of the viewer); what is there outside the painting that attracts his attention? These questions would all be in vain, were it not for a quandary that for me has become a fascinating enigma, which is the result of all those contrasting glances, and which becomes evident upon reflection: the child is the only one who is *seeing* something; all the other eyes are *looking*, but they do not see.

I will leave aside the coldness with which the Madonna relates to the child – the child seems to be sitting on air, not on his mother's lap – for it seems to me more interesting to dwell on the effect the artist achieves with the three separate colors: the texture and color of the Madonna and the child's skin remind us of wax; the bright red of the six chubby angels holding on to the throne, of a candle flame; and finally, the three blue-gray angels in the background of the painting, of the penumbra in the corners beyond the bright halo of candle light.

As I am considering whether the roundest forms are near the warmest chromatic arrangements, I hear a dry cough behind me.

"We are closing, sir."

I turn on my heels, and see Denis smiling apologetically. I look around the room: I see only the museum attendant and me, no one else. The light that filters into the room has the thinness of old honey. I don't know how long I have been staring at Fouquet's painting.

I start apologizing, but he won't let me continue.

"Take this, I would be very grateful if you would accept my invitation," and he hands me a piece of paper with an address written on it. "It's not so far away from here. I could invite you to a restaurant, but we will be able to speak more leisurely in my home. Would eight o'clock suit you? I can't make it earlier, I'm afraid; it takes quite a while to activate the museum's alarm system."

Denis leaves the room before I am able to answer him.

I am not a great believer in divine providence, or in blind Cupid's fateful arrows, or in predestination; but, if I turned my back to Denis' mad whim, wouldn't I, in fact, be going against my beliefs? I've already made up my mind: I really have nothing better to do, so I go to my hotel, where I have just enough time to take a shower and change my clothes, and, without further ado, head towards the address on the piece of paper, fuelled by a desire to learn more about his strange request.

At eight o'clock sharp I am standing in front of the door to Denis' apartment.

It is difficult at first to identify the man with the gaudy flowery shirt who opens the door as the museum attendant in the blue uniform. The uniform dulled and flattened out all the physical characteristics of the man I met at the museum (he blended into the background, even if I have attempted to humanize him by calling him Denis); the flowery shirt, on the other hand, distances him too much from the man under the uniform, and realizing that – and noticing that his smile and all his mannerisms are sort of flowery, perhaps? – has made me feel slightly uneasy.

He has guided me to an impersonal living room with few decorations. "The room of someone who lives alone," is what occurs to me, for Denis' living room bears all the traces of someone who has rejected family or company as well as decorations and other superfluities.

After filling two glasses with *trappistine*, Denis offers me one:

"Do you know it?" he asks me, lifting his glass in the air. "No, it isn't a very well-known drink. They make it like Armagnac, but with fewer herbs. It's a good appetizer, it stimulates the taste buds."

We toast, and sit at the table. He removes a longish vase that blocks our view of each other's eyes, and starts ladling onion soup onto my plate from a soup tureen. I taste the soup, and as soon as I compliment it he starts to speak, almost spilling over, like an overflowing fountain.

"I see that Fouquet's Madonna interests you, then. I would have sworn you were a journalist when I saw you walk into the room, but realized immediately that the way you were looking at the painting had nothing to do with the quick, superficial way journalists have of only looking at the most obvious things. Nor are you one of those poseurs who pretend to be extremely knowledgeable; that's also evident. The differences between visitors are made clear by the manner in which they pause to view the painting: you, for example, let your eyes rest at the core of the composition, at a very precise point in the painting, and from there you have drawn each and every one of your findings. Before concluding anything, you always go back to the core, like a bee that flies back to the sweetest flower after sampling all the others. You're a teacher, aren't you? Or perhaps you are a painter, too? Have you ever been to the Berlin-Dahlem museum? Never? Tut, tut, tut! Then you don't know the story of Fouquet's painting – or do you?

I can't get a word in edgeways: the museum attendant's lips barely open, but sibilant sounds escape through them continually, while he ignores all my attempts to participate in the conversation. His hands, though, move more and more histrionically: he points at several of the painting's invisible parts with a fork, as if he had it in front of him, and immediately after at the public – me – with the brisk persuasive movement of a fisherman throwing a net.

"That Madonna of the delectable breast was a whore," continues Denis, "a courtesan, the darling of Charles VII, his lover, a concubine who liked to share her bed with one or many men concurrently, with everybody, please forgive me all this obscenity. Her name was Agnès Sorel, and she appears in Fouquet's painting in the same way as in every other depiction of her: with her left breast exposed. Everybody would agree with me if I said motherhood is the meaning of the bare breast in Fouquet's painting, but why is it that this naked breast, again and again, this very left breast, appears in paintings that have nothing to do with motherhood or anything remotely connected with it?" asks Denis, directing his eyes from his imaginary painting to me with an expression full of hope, as if I might be the one to hold the answer to his puzzle.

"Unfortunately, I can't guess at his intended meaning unless I try to unearth some of the clues that lie outside the orbit of the author's artistic urges," I say, just to say something.

His eyes fill with light, as if he has just remembered something important, but he smacks his lips and gets up after making an apologetic gesture with his hand. He leaves the room, and a short while later returns holding a bottle of *Chateaux Margoux*.

"What do you think?" asks Denis, showing me the bottle. "It's been in the fridge for years, awaiting an occasion such as this."

He goes through the whole process with much ceremony, uncorking the bottle, pouring the wine, swirling it in his glass, smelling it, barely tasting it with the tip of his tongue.

"What do you think?" he asks again.

As I am debating whether to answer that it is a pity to allow such good wine to turn to vinegar by letting it age, Denis drops the subject, and I gather that that was the object of the pause and the bottle of wine: to whet my appetite for knowledge in this crucible of respite.

The gratefulness we owe to our hosts requires me to massage the museum attendant's ego:

"I don't know, but it would seem to me that you are bursting with the need to discover something, something to add to what you already know and no one else knows: am I wrong?"

Denis did not need much encouragement to continue speaking.

"*Ma petite pomme*, is how the king used to call Agnès' breast; were you aware of this?"

Denis breathes deeply and stares at me, awaiting my response. I keep my mouth shut, because I don't know whether he is expecting me to come up with an explanation, or if he is indulging in one of those theatrical silences, those brief pauses, in fact, during which the audience, thinking that it is time for the intermission, clap.

I wait for him, then; I wait, and don't bat an eyelid.

My attitude encourages Denis to give free rein to his passion, and he continues speaking, slower than he did earlier, providing me with innumerable well-known details: that this painting in which Agnès Sorel poses as the Madonna is part of a diptych; that the knight Etienne Chevalier, who used to be the king's accountant, was depicted in the other half; that Etienne is kneeling and staring at Agnès the Madonna...

"The piece which shows Etienne Chevalier kneeling is now at the National Museum of Berlin. No one has been able to explain why they separated the two parts of the diptych. And that, sir, is almost everything we know," says Denis finally, with a frown.

I could have sworn that the museum attendant's life was in danger, if it wasn't that the subject of his story was so far removed from the present.

"And?" I ask him. "What's worrying you?"

Denis directs his proud eyes from his empty glass to mine, and from there to the bottle. He starts to pour from the bottle of *Chateaux Margoux*. Placing the palm of my hand over my glass, I indicate I will not have another drink.

Denis starts whispering all of a sudden, as if he were afraid that someone else might hear:

"They poisoned Agnès, sir. You knew that, didn't you?"

The bewilderment in Denis' eyes made me think of the demented flight of two birds frightened by a shot.

"The son of Charles VII killed her, Louis XI, you must know that, too," he corroborates this with a serious voice, rather than question my knowledge. "Louis XI used Agnès' cuckolding of the king as an excuse to take revenge and poison the girl. Do you understand? It was an excuse! But why? That is the question: why?"

Denis' manner gets more and more grandiloquent, and, feeling uncomfortable, I try a little joke to ease up the atmosphere:

"Because he wanted to punish all the mistresses and mistresses-in-waiting of his court, why otherwise? 'You better tread carefully, my little whores, look what you risk!' That was the message – why else would he kill her?" I say to him jokingly, like a dilettante art critic.

"Cold, cold, that kind of speculation is baseless," explains Denis, his eyes shining crazily. "Why did Fouquet break his diptych in two? That is the question and the question has to be answered, don't you think?"

With all the time and ease I can muster I give him all the possible explanations that occur to me: Agnès' clandestine love – even though she was the king's mistress she felt a fiery passion for Etienne – was made visible to everyone through the diptych, and to break it in two might have been a way to signal condemnation and punishment. Hadn't Fouquet, in fact, portrayed the king as a laughable figure and a cuckold by putting Etienne on the second part of the diptych?

"It's not bad, you think that Fouquet was afraid of the revenge this laughable and cuckolded king might wreak on him, I understand," says Denis, considering the different aspects of the train of thought. "But that just leads us back to the unavoidable question, don't you think?"

I don't think that or anything else, and unlike before, I give him a doubtful look.

Denis doesn't like my attitude, and continues to question me with sharp, icy anger:

"Who is the child on Agnès' lap? Isn't the child on the Madonna's lap as real as Agnès Sorel and Etienne Chevalier – the son of a highly-born man, perhaps?"

"Let's say the child is the king's bastard, and consequently, the brother of Louis XI" – I said, retaining a trace of my dilettantish manner: "'You, Fouquet, have crossed the line; be careful, the king is going to make porridge out of you if he sees the painting,' people at the court probably told him. Even Fouquet, with his artistic temperament, was like you or me: he feared the king (do not forget that Agnès had died by poisoning); he respected him (thanks to the king his social and economic standing were assured). But he also got a thrill out of stirring things up, he could imagine the lords and ladies of the court staring at the painting and saying: 'Look, look, doesn't the little mite look just like prince Louis?' (We should not forget that Fouquet was, above all, an artist)."

He signals a 'no' with his head.

"That baby is Chevalier's son," he says, pale as pale can be, so much so it looks like the drink has made him feel ill.

"Why do you say that?"

"Because he is looking at a currently invisible spot in the second part of the diptych."

"I don't understand…"

"Who is there in that second part of the diptych, kneeling down in that precise spot? Etienne Chevalier, the king's accountant; you said it yourself a moment ago. I would say that the child sitting on the Madonna's lap is looking at his father, at Etienne."

Imbecile, I am a total imbecile, how could I not have noticed something so blatantly obvious? I think, giving myself a metaphorical slap for being so blind.

"*Hèlas!*" I applaud Denis' deduction, "*Hèlas!* Not bad at all, good idea!"

I thought he would enjoy my appreciation, but to my surprise, he gets angry, and looks like he's beginning to think he's wasting his time with me.

"I thought you were a sensitive man, sir."

I apologize, attempting the humblest tone I am capable of. I say that I've been blind, blind to an incredible degree. I ask him to go on with his explanation.

"You don't realize the reason why Fouquet brought the painting to Berlin, do you? You don't realize," Denis bursts out uncontrollably.

And what if Fouquet himself had split the painting in two and sent it to Berlin, was the thought that crossed my mind, but before I could say anything, Denis was assailed by what looked like a terrible thought, as if he'd forgotten something of the utmost importance.

"Eleven o'clock! I'm sorry, sir, I'm sorry! I have to leave," says Denis in a cavernous whisper.

I look at my watch. It's nowhere near eleven.

As fast as he can, Denis puts on a blue jacket very similar to his uniform over his flowery shirt. On the jacket's lapel a small silver insignia with the museum's logo shines brightly. As he is getting dressed, he tells me that he takes a stroll to the museum every night, to check that everything is in order.

His amazing change of attitude provides me with the perfect excuse to return to the hotel – with the sudden interruption, dinner is abandoned there and then – and I try to make things easier for Denis: of course he must do his duty; he shouldn't worry about me; it's a splendid night and I'll just walk back to the hotel…

"I think I understood before that your hotel is near the museum. It'll be quicker if I take you…" he says in an excessively forceful tone that blocks all possible routes of escape.

We leave the building and get into a small car parked in the street. There are road works around Denis' street that force us to take a couple of detours, which in turn provokes him to mumble a couple of colorful expletives. After that, he doesn't say anything else until we reach the gates of the museum.

Denis gets out of the car.

"Thanks for everything," I say. But I don't think he hears me, for he has already disappeared among the trees that surround the museum.

I head towards the hotel, reflecting on the strange things that have happened to me in the last few hours. Even if there is a definite chill to the night air, it is nice to be walking.

Less than five minutes after I leave Denis in front of the museum, I hear fast-approaching footsteps behind me. Seconds later, Denis' voice calls out:

"Wait, wait!"

He is out of breath when he catches up with me:

"Everything is under control. *My* Madonna is safe. Did you know that even a bird flying into the museum could set the alarm off? But nothing like that has ever happened. And even if it did happen, it's not a bird that I live in fear of, but some crazy person hiding in the toilets, taking advantage of the dark night…" He leaves the sentence unfinished and picks up the conversation where he'd previously left it, while pointing at a bar squeezed in between the houses: "Let us continue our conversation. What about that one? Any place will do."

The name above the *boîte* Denis is pointing at shines in neon red: *Paradise.*

I tell him I am tired.

He holds me by the elbow, and we walk into the dimly-lit *boîte,* after crossing a dark lengthy corridor that smells like an Arabian marketplace.

The decadent décor of the *boîte* attempts to recreate Paradise in its Hawaiian version – imitating its atmosphere, natural surroundings and light.

Just as we are about to sit down at a one-legged table under a dusty plastic palm tree, two girls approach us. The room is so full of smoke that I can't really comment on their appearance, other than to say that their tits are practically hanging out.

Having resigned myself to the fact that I wasn't going to be able to get rid of Denis, I said it was my round and ordered two drinks.

"Get these two a drink too," he says to me. Then he turns to them: "Please my darlings, take your drinks and leave us; can you not see we wish to talk about our business?"

When the girls leave – not without giving us a scornful look – Denis picks up the subject as if he'd never left it, and starts talking as fervently as he did in his apartment:

"What is Fouquet's painting? A Madonna. Why did he remove the part with Etienne on it? Because it got in the way of the Madonna."

"In the... way?" I ask, after overcoming the sense of unreality that has overtaken me – I find it hard to believe we are discussing the painting in a place like this.

"In the way, yes, it was an embarrassment, it was uncomfortable. Fouquet wanted to portray the Madonna. He chose a beautiful model named Agnès Sorel, probably the most beautiful woman in the court. But real people must give up their reality in favor of the object they're representing; it is written. However, at the time, what people saw in the diptych was Agnès the harlot and Etienne the avaricious lecher, instead of the Madonna and the devout member of the court. Even doing away with Etienne's section, what did the painter gain? Agnès was too alive. *In presenti*. The face of a royal whore ate away all the substance and the glory from the symbol of the Madonna! You should know, sir, that it is essential for any symbol, whatever it may be, that all worldly references used in its creation are erased, that they disappear.

Just as our bodies assimilate the foods we eat. Otherwise it ceases to be a symbol."

It crosses my mind that Denis must have taken those words from some sleek handbook or other. I have often heard similar arguments. It seems to me that, ever since we are as free to go to an art museum as we are to vote, people think that voting (in order to decide the future of their nation) does not differ much from judging a work of art (because they think taste is linked to democracy).

"Do you think that's why Fouquet removed the second part, to reinforce the symbol? Then why didn't he make it disappear?"

Denis rests his hand on mine.

"How could he possibly make it disappear? A diptych painted in the manner of the Italian master Piero de la Francesca by a French painter of his generation? Oh, the artist's soul! Artists would rather feel the fires of hell burning their insides than follow the call of the heavens. But, sir, I would have thought that you knew these things about artists."

"So, that's why he took it to Berlin… In order not to betray his artistic soul."

"Of course; why else? Consider that Berlin is not so far away now as it was in Fouquet's time, but back then he probably thought that by sending that part of the diptych there, he was effectively removing a sizeable part of the problem: by sending that second, compromising section of the diptych to Berlin he avoided the king's jealousy, silenced the speculation about the Madonna and the child, and, at the same time, saved the painting from certain destruction."

I think I hear him hiccup as he pronounces the last words. He looks a wreck. Just as I am about to ask him what's wrong with him, he grasps my hand for the second time:

"Everybody saw Agnès in the painting, they still see Agnès, the loose girl who hopped from bed to bed, and not the Madonna. You can't do that to the poor Madonna, you can't do that to her!"

And then Denis makes me the most amazing proposal I've heard in my entire life:

"Go to Berlin, sir; please, I beg you – for the sake of all that's precious. If you could destroy Etienne Chevalier's section, then Agnès Sorel, without her lover, would lose her glow and the Madonna would recover hers, which she so badly needs. I would go to Berlin myself, but someone must stay here to look after the Madonna, you have seen that even a little bird can put everything at risk. I wouldn't ask anything like this of you if it weren't that I've seen you look at the Madonna with such grateful deference and respect..."

"Even if I went to Berlin and destroyed Etienne Chevalier's painting... What about all the other paintings of Agnès Sorel?" I wanted to know. "There will always be several paintings of her around and someday someone is bound to make a link between Agnès' naked breast and your Madonna..."

"We have quite a bit of work ahead of us, sir," answers Denis, grinding his teeth.

KARLOS LINAZASORO (Tolosa, 1962)

I was born in Tolosa, and I have been a librarian in the town's public library for a long time. I studied Basque Philology at university, but I don't teach. I have written four collections of short stories: *Eldarnioak* (1991, *The Eldarnios*), *Zer gerta ere* (1994, *Whatever Happened?*), *Ez balego beste mundurik* (2000, *If There Wasn't Another World*), and *Ipuin errotikoak* (2001, *Erotic Tales*). I have also written four volumes of poetry, a theatre play, and quite a few books for children and young people. Poetry and the short story are my favorite genres; the novel doesn't fit in my world-view. I believe that writing makes me free, but I don't know if I love freedom. These are some of my teachers: Kafka, Borges, Cortázar, Felisberto Hernández, Beckett, Rulfo, Saki, Wilcock, Piñera, Chekhov, Hrabal, Mrozek, Bernhard, Anderson Imbert, Arreola, Poe...

I like short stories that make use of fantasy, have a touch of playfulness, are splattered with the violence of life, chal-

lenge the reader and are powerful, suggestive, full of the unex-
pected; I also think, at the same time, that in short stories
humor and irony are a must; for they are the most appropriate
weapons for combating human tragedies, alienation, solitude,
or the absurdity of life, because they offer distance and protection. The short story can transgress all laws, but has its own
rules: within them there's still room for you to really be free, in
the reign of allegory and metaphor.

The Derailment

by

KARLOS LINAZASORO

Translated by Amaia Gabantxo

By the time the accident happened my friend Cioran had sent me to the depths of despair. He'd behaved like a heartless pig, despicably. The carriage crumpled like an accordion, and the two flies on the window stopped copulating. Distant alarm bells could be heard then, their whine a touch military, or a touch inappropriate, I couldn't decide. I opened my eyes, disoriented, probably as a consequence of the sweat that was breaking profusely from my head, and I saw, with gray-blue eyes, the book that had fallen from my hands covered in blood, and the truth is that I was even happy. But that happiness didn't last long; my traveling companion – an elderly man with white combed-back hair and limpid, shining eyes – lay dead on the gray floor two rows away from me. He was dead, with a frozen smile on his face. He held a pair of expensive glasses with his right hand, because he was missing the left one, as he himself had told me a few minutes earlier as we crossed a squalid field. I was pointing out, at the time, the spots on the horizon where taciturn specimens applied themselves to some unhurried ploughing, composing as they moved truly haunting human shapes. Just as I was describing the scene, he told me to shut up, that he was missing his left arm, and that his disability often ruined his mood. Because I have a tendency to look not just at the positive, but even at the comic side of things, I asked him, giggling slightly but with all due respect, which mood he was referring to, a metaphysical mood or some other one, that I was but a poor provincial writer and could he please explain it to me more slowly. He got all teary and sad, and started parting his hair with laudable dexterity. Afterwards, he started laughing uncontrollably and I remember that for a few moments the whole carriage laughed at his laughter. Could it be that his cruel and spasmodic laughter was the reason for the accident?

The old man, of course, didn't answer my question. After we'd laughed and passed the field we became friends. The train was swerving violently, like a gigantic, broken lizard, and the old man – who, whether out of shame or for some other reason that I could not begin to guess at, had not told me his name – had to hold his dentures in place quite a few times in a very short space of time. Despite the disagreeableness of the situation, we became friends. Our relationship was courteous, given that we were facing each other, and he told me that he was a teacher, and a libertine widower. It was midday and unbearably hot, and we informed the ticket collector that the air-conditioning was not working, and trying to hint at the same time, ever so discreetly, that they probably hadn't switched it on. The ticket collector punched our tickets for the fifth time, and disappeared like some scary ghost. We dwelled very briefly on his astounding disappearance; both of us, I'm sure, thought the same, even if we didn't say anything. The train had stopped swerving a little, but the heat was still intense, and the old man was overtaken by a heavy stupor. He fell asleep with a smile,

with impeccable trousers, with his outsized hand, and I
took Cioran's book out of my satchel again, with a slight
disgust and sticky hands.

Half an hour sufficed to send me to the depths of
despair. Fear had taken hold of me. I saw two flies copulating against the glass, rakishly, lovelessly. I looked out of
the window for the last time and chose to see – even if I
can't remember them anymore – birds in flames, paper
flowers and perhaps an angel in the shade of the earthly
lime trees. And just then, the accident. An explosion dis-
rupted the calm afternoon, and the intense heat, and the
little nap, and the reading. A collision, a derailment perhaps, a complication we would never understand. This
precisely, I swear, is what came to my mind first. But no;
it was none of those things: neither collision, nor derailment, nor complication, even if I didn't completely grasp
this until later. At the beginning it seemed to me that it
was an accident, a vile, despicable accident. The reasons
for it were unknown, but any of the three I have mentioned would do. In any case, this wasn't the first puzzle
I faced after the accident. The first one was to worry
about our friend the old man; the one I'd found dead two
rows away from me, with a frozen smile on his silver
mouth. I brought him towards me forcefully, with all my
strength, thinking that he was only asleep, and realized,
to my astonishment, that the body lying on the gray floor
was not the body of a man, but a rag doll. Incredibly well
made, that's for sure, but not an ounce of blood in its
veins. It was nothing but rags and sawdust, a bundle of
lies; I was offended, and my soul hurt.

This disagreeable surprise dramatically altered my
perception of the events. Suddenly, I felt a bleak empti-
ness in my stomach, a fat, secret pain, and I vomited a

revolting greenish water all over the insentient body. I
stood up. With a certain aloofness, as slowly as I could, I
looked at the rest of the travelers. They were all seated in
their places, as if what had just happened had nothing to
do with them; obstinately ignoring the facts. I lit a cigarette and a blind man said: "What's happening? What's
happening?" No one answered and the atmosphere
turned very uncomfortable. I smoked my cigarette
amidst coughs and grotesque facial expressions. I thought
that if all those travelers remained so calmly seated, totally turned in on themselves and moving their heads one
way and the other, smiling without showing their teeth,
it must be because they really believed there hadn't been
an accident; and, even if something had really happened,
it didn't quite qualify as an accident, even less as something vile and despicable, as I had initially assumed,
clearly – I realize now – fuelled by my reading and my
natural tendency toward hyperbole and exaggeration. In
the event, I decided to remember things coolly, with the
certainty of distance, and after a while I realized I had
gone too far in my conclusions, and that all the chaos
and obscenity had not really taken place. Yes, of course,
the carriage had crumpled like an accordion, but precisely because it was like an accordion, it had returned to its
usual shape, as if a gigantic pump had blown air into it,
and, for that reason, apart from the odd cranial collision
or minor lesion, everything stayed the same, as if nothing
had happened.

But it was obvious that something had happened:
nothing vile or despicable, but something that, although
insignificant in appearance, was in truth of great importance and in fact irrevocable. It looked as though everything was the same, but everything had changed. Like

the river's flow, which is always one but never the same. I went through many hypotheses, commonsensical ones, measured ones, and the result of my ruminations was a word that left a bitter taste in the mouth: conspiracy. The word left my mouth, gained substance, and swelled like a mother's breast. I pronounced it in order to never again be able to fathom it: it had become a green dove with a voice like the moon. A conspiracy, I repeated, pondering each letter. But why? I asked myself: why us? I didn't know the answer, I couldn't even begin to comprehend what the purpose of it was or who was pulling the strings behind the scenes (an individual? a sect?). I would have been grateful for answers to all these questions, it goes without saying, for it is important to know one's enemy in order be as ready for him as possible, but I realized immediately that I would never find out the answers. Not ever. Without a shadow of a doubt I also knew, instantly, that the conspiracy was part of a plot, a sabotage plan, one that had irreversible consequences. What drove me to these conclusions? What solid evidence did I have to back up such extraordinary utterances?

As was my habit – or rather, as my anxiety dictated – I was trying to work out an explanation, when I heard Schubert. I recognized him immediately; a deep, boundless grief enveloped me, informing me that I was alone. I recovered my senses as well as I could; I looked at the blind man, at the child who, with his mother, was reading one of those lovely fairytales, and at the young couple. They were satisfying the most ancient of fires, without shame, like jungle beasts, fearless of finding each other's eyes in the dark or at the very valley of death. The girl said: "take my lips, devour my lips," like that, in the same way a doll would repeat a stupid sentence, without feeling; and the boy, who was younger than me and yet already scandalously bold was trying with all his might to satisfy his beloved's desire, while he stared at a group of pensioners with gold membership cards. They stared right back at the boy, thinking that they could satisfy the girl's desire so much better than that poor inexperienced lad; but by then the boy was devouring another pair of lips, lips as soft and sweet as an open flower. And just then Schubert ended, and I stopped looking out in order to look into myself; I was alone and had to explain to myself in no uncertain terms why I had voiced the word conspiracy, why I had allowed that frightening word to escape, a word which seemed to have been written down by an anonymous hand, at once strangely cruel and familiar. I sat down; a plane pierced the bruised sky, and that vision made me feel like the shipwreck abandoned on a desert island, even if I couldn't guess why. I lit another cigarette, and at that precise moment the blind man said in a rasping voice: "What's happening? What's happening?" I caught sight of the *No Smoking* sign above me, and the blind man's sarcasm dawned on me; he was telling me not to smoke. I pretended not to notice, of course; and I went even further: taking advantage of the pseudo-mystical atmosphere we were experiencing in the carriage, I decided to extinguish my cigarette butt on the blind man's hand, so that he got it clear in his head who was boss. And that's what I did; he didn't utter the smallest of complaints, and for that reason I thought that either he was soft in the head, or he was doing it as a form of sophisticated revenge. On the other hand, I considered, the blind man might well be a worthless masochist. And what if he was? What if the blind guy was a masochistic pig? I didn't think twice (I have always been a dynamic, quick-witted guy): I took off my belt and whipped him thirty or forty times, without anger but confidently, now on the head, now on the arms and legs. He didn't complain once, not one small whimper came out of him, and so, feeling totally bored, I gave up on administering the punishment, although I was still unclear about whether the blind man had enjoyed the whipping or not. The fact that I couldn't clear up this doubt, I must confess, made me feel quite faint.

Minutes went by, not too slowly and not too quickly, just the same as ever, inexorably. The only thing I'd like to establish with this statement is that life went on, that desire was still more or less eternal, and that poetry and the snow will always be innocent. Small consolation, in any case, because life in there had nothing to do with the inner life; it was nothing but a memory. And from that life that was but a memory, from those pages soiled with wine and blood and small happiness and often sterile seed (even if I had initially closed my eyes with the secret hope that all those stories had nothing to do with me), eventually I dissected the truth, after I'd put together all the evidence that had presented itself to me from the very first moment of my journey until the clouds parted. But, oh, how wrong I was to be hopeful! First of all, the old man made of rags and sawdust had died, without having ever lived. That shock made me open my eyes: I had befriended a puppet who was only a voice. Then I realized there had never been an accident: our carriage had come loose, we'd landed on a field in the middle of nowhere. The event wasn't such a great technical impossibility: we were the last carriage. And now we had nobody in front of us. And all windows and doors were hermetically sealed, too *thoroughly* closed even, I thought to myself after a close and concise inspection; there were no hammers or pointy tools, nor any travelers who might be carrying any: it was totally impossible, as a result, to break a window in order to get out and get some help.

Mulling over the events in my head, I started unraveling the thread, trying to make sense of it all: between the clouds, between the dreams I'd thought weren't my own, cow-like figures appeared, I could now see them quite clearly; they took shape, and turned into gigantic murals that hurt my eyes. I couldn't escape the realization anymore: how could I not have known that the accident wasn't a vile and despicable event, but that simply, if rather incredibly, our carriage had come off? Hadn't I realized a while ago that the one-armed grandpa was nothing but an evil rag doll? Hadn't I seen with my own eyes his straw heart? And incidentally, hadn't I said – told the rag doll himself, in my amazement – that the ticket inspector was a scary ghost? Why did he punch our tickets five times? Why did the train take so many detours from its daily route, using the excuse of works on the line, strikes and engine failures, when nothing of the sort had happened in the last twenty years? Where were we now? On the deserted railway line of a long-abandoned mining town? Why weren't any cars or trains passing by? Why was there not one single house, factory, or sign of life? Those enormous wheat fields that embraced the horizon, was it their destiny to become pastures of forgetfulness? Why did no one have any luggage? Did they know their train was going nowhere? Why did the ticket collector – who, in fact wasn't the usual one, but someone taller and more shameless and certainly more libertine, and whom I had never seen before – wish me a good journey, if he didn't know me? Was he just being courteous? Of course not; the cynical tone he'd used left no room for doubt. He was telling me: "I don't know where you're going, you stupid man, but this will be your last journey."

I gave up unraveling the thread, trying to make sense of it all, looking at that gigantic mural pregnant with questions for a little while. The field looked like it was about to melt under the flaming sun. The heat was unbearable, yet no one was sweating; it looked as if no one had noticed the sort of trap we'd fallen into, or perhaps they did realize, and were just calmly waiting for the arrival of some Herculean rescue force. In any case, the scene was breathtaking: no one moved from their seats, no one – apart from the blind man – asked any questions, no one was crying with anxiety, because of the lack of air or just out of extreme fear. I realized then that it is impossible to remain so passive in the face of imminent disgrace or death, that such madness had to be nothing other than clear evidence of a con; in other words, that all the travelers *knew already* that they would be freed, or, if not, that if things got really bad they wouldn't have to face any consequences. From that I deduced that all these travelers had to be either impartial or enemies; if impartial, only because they had been hired – or perhaps forced or even kidnapped – to enact this farce, or rather, this tragedy; if enemies, only because they may have been ordered to finish me off right away or in some awful twisted way. This disagreeable suspicion grabbed hold of me, and not only did I become more and more persuaded that it was true, but I realized it might even be dangerous to consider my fellow travelers merely impartial to my fate. In this particular case, impartiality – either chosen freely or imposed by means of fear – was unjustifiable, both for its cruelty and its inconceivable consequences. It was clearly a conspiracy plotted against me, by then I had no doubt at all this was the case. Why, though? Why did I deserve such a sentence? Was I rich and powerful? Had I killed someone? Had I broken any laws? Had I denied God? The answer to all these questions was clearly no. Also clear, I now saw, was the reason: I had been sentenced for being humble, righteous, fair, cheerful, honest and dull; for believing in humanity and its goodness; for thinking that innocence existed and that friendship could not be bought or sold; for fighting in favor of the unity of countries and praising the purity of love; in other words, for being at one with my ethical and aesthetic notions, and for demonstrating that oneness in my books. Or perhaps – I thought, frightened – it was because he, or they, didn't like my short stories? Was it accurate or even acceptable to think that they wanted to finish me off just because of my romantic stories, my dirges, satirical quatrains or lyrical poems? Can the human soul contain so much hatred?

I remember that the notion of the *human soul* made me laugh, and profiting from my advantageous position, I decided there and then to burst out laughing right in front of my venomous enemies. It was a long, sonorous cackle, a very realistic one, sprinkled with a touch of psychosis. I didn't achieve anything, however; not one of the travelers showed a shred of emotion, no one changed their attitude, no one was annoyed, no one said a word. They knew their script very well, and they weren't about to start improvising. Fear had taken hold of them, a thick, ancestral terror that sped through their thoughts like a victorious viper. This ultimate failure altered my philosophy of life, my perception of the world, the poetics of my art and writing forever. As from now, as far as I was concerned, man was innately evil, love and togetherness did not exist, nor, more acutely, did innocence and happiness. Not even of the soul. And then I ceased to laugh, and understood that only by means of torture would I get a confession out of that bunch of mercenaries. It was clear, however, that they would not let themselves be tortured that easily, and at the same time, that they were aware of the possibility of it happening, and of how to act if it did happen. Most likely things would go wrong and they'd do me in, beat me to death like a miserable dog; but, I thought immediately afterwards, what was the use of a life such as this? Wasn't I already dead, a living-dead?

Since this was how things were, I put my plan into practice as soon as I could. I had a small but strong reason, which had very little to do with anything military and a lot with everything poetic. Hatred made me blind. I stood under the *No Smoking* sign again, and lit a cigarette with a half-meter flame. The blind man, with all the bad grace in the world, said: "What's going on? What's going on?" And that's how I concluded that the blind guy could see better than I, and that, without a shadow of a doubt, his little cantilena was an important signal. I was glad he repeated it, because it gave me a valid excuse to remove my belt again and give him a thorough whipping, without anger this time, but confidently, now on the head, now on the arms and legs. But – damn! – he went down without a sound, and without confessing to the Machiavellian reasons for the conspiracy; he escaped from my grasp, I killed him forever, and I felt a profound happiness inside me, a blameless peace, the sort of tranquility that knowing you have one less enemy gives you. Crossing that line made me stronger, and I felt my remaining enemies getting weaker: I felt cruel and exacting, and that's how they saw me. I could be just as mercenary as they were, or more. And, to be honest, they were so shocked and stunned to see so much blood that they were left powerless to show any sign of innocence or togetherness or love towards the deceased, or any sign of hatred or condemnation towards me. I had them under my control; but it wasn't a good idea to celebrate my triumph quite yet. I realized I had a long, arduous job ahead of me.

Dusk was falling slowly, like a leaf lit up with stars. A wheat field entered my sphere of vision, naked and immense in my window: no one had ever crossed it. I closed my eyes and cried. Later, after a short interval, in the distance that I used to love looking into, in the horizon speckled with darkness, some red lights, dark, blinking and familiar, got lost and then reappeared in the blind, distant sky, getting closer and closer, so much closer now, and yet so vile and so despicable.

PELLO LIZARRALDE (Zumarraga, 1956)

I was born in Zumarraga in 1956. Most of the people there had just recently abandoned their scythes and hoes. Our father became a truck driver. I've spent many hours on the highway and on trains. I've had some crazy dreams, but never that I would be a "professional writer."

The magazines *Zeruko Argia* and *Argia* gave me the opportunity to write and learn, and the magazine *Ustela* gave me the opportunity to publish. I have since published six books — *Sargori* (*Heat Wave*) in 1994 and *Un ange passe: Isilaldietan* (*An Angel Passes: In Moments of Silence*) in 1998 — and I don't know what to say about what I've written. My life would be lessened if I were forced to give up writing, but it would be unbearable if I had to give up reading.

I have come across some very kind people among Basque writers and lovers of literature, but I have few kindred spirits among them.

When I hear that I'm a writer, it embarrasses me less than it used to. I want to continue writing, but I'm not in any hurry.

Awkward Silence

by

PELLO LIZARRALDE

Translated by Elizabeth Macklin and Linda White

They were stuck a third of a mile from the mountain pass. Nothing was moving forward or backward. Some thirty vehicles sat all in a line facing the same direction in the middle of the blinding white of the highland meadow. Cars facing the other way were on the other side of the pass, forced to wait by policemen in red berets.

There was occasional movement among the cars and trucks at the end of the line as they made efforts to move the last few yards up the incline onto the short stretch of flat road.

Kurt had just got onto level ground and could inch a bit forward. But the driver of the semi in front of him put out an arm and signaled him to stop. Kurt braked, then half a minute later, he turned off his engine. He repeated the gesture to the drivers of a big rig and three cars that he could see behind him in the rearview mirror. He sighed and leaned his arms and forehead on the steering wheel. Then he reached backward into the sleeper for the thermos. The coffee was bitter and tepid, and it didn't do the trick. He opened his window and emptied the thermos, turning the snow and ice in the middle of the road a coffee color.

After a bit, Kurt put on his sunglasses and opened the door of the cab. He checked for a clean patch of asphalt, then jumped down and took a look ahead.

"Oh, shit!" He swore in German between clenched teeth and kicked loose a chunk of dirty ice from his rig.

The jack-knifed semi was two hundred yards up the road and twenty-odd drivers were lurching toward it on foot in the left lane. Kurt cast his gaze over the dark figures making their way, alone or in pairs.

No movement was visible beyond them, but Kurt knew at once from the smoke that hid the semi from view that things were not quiet up there. He shoved his hands into his jacket pockets and headed off with the others.

He decided to walk in the left-hand ditch because there was less ice there. He looked around, then paused. He spied a rig from his country on the right. On the left was a snow-covered field and a flood of silence. Alongside the ditch there was underbrush and the sparkle of droplets frozen to its branches.

Kurt moved beyond the brush to get a look at faint bird tracks in the snow. After a breather, he glanced at the sky, then started off again.

The smell of smoke and the sound of engines intensified. Kurt slowed alongside the truck and planted himself behind the crowd gathered there. The semi was English and people on the other side were helping, giving directions to the driver. From his position, Kurt could glimpse their legs and feet. Sometimes they shouted, voices tense.

Kurt noticed a fellow German just a few yards away, revealed by the flag sewn on his leather sleeve. He wore a wool cap and was very young. He stared wide-eyed.

Some of the drivers began moving off. One of their voices could be heard over the noise. "What the hell does he have chains for?"

"You can never tell with these foreigners," added another, biting back his anger. "All night down there waiting to move, and when we get going, this. Fuck!"

Kurt had learned enough of the language on previous trips to understand the gist of what he heard. He approached his compatriot and introduced himself. They shook hands and stood talking, gesturing from time to time at the ice beneath the semi.

They decided they'd be there for a couple of hours and walked back the way they'd come. At the young driver's rig, he told Kurt he had zero desire to leave his cab. He was going to get some sleep. Kurt said goodbye and went on to his own truck. All the vehicles in the line had their engines off. Fierce gusts of wind brought somber sounds off the snow-covered plain.

Kurt took out his keys and locked the door of his truck. He stood for a moment at his tailgate and looked over the lineup of vehicles. He counted fifteen between himself and the bottom of the slope below. He started downhill.

"Hey, excuse me."

The dark-haired girl in the white car had her window half down and was speaking from the driver's seat. The blonde girl on the passenger side was looking at Kurt. He made his way back to them.

"Will it take long up there?" the brunette asked as he approached. "A long time?" she rephrased her question.

"A couple of hours." Kurt tipped his hand back and forth to mean more or less.

"What happened?" asked the brunette. Her companion cut her off. "Leave him be, he's not from here."

The brunette turned and thanked him. Then she gave a weary laugh before rolling up the window. Kurt raised a hand by way of farewell.

Farther down the slope, some cars had their engines running. The passengers were wearing jackets. A few yards farther along there were beeches beside the road, and the north wind was more noticeable. From the shaded ravine came a far-off whistle.

From behind him, Kurt heard, "What are you doing, girl — watch it!"

The blonde had the brunette by the arm, and the brunette had one knee on the ground. When she managed to get up, they spoke to each other but Kurt couldn't understand what they said. He stood watching until they started down the slope again. Then he went on his way, moving obviously more slowly. From the sounds behind him, he knew the girls' footing was uncertain and that they were falling farther and farther behind.

He decided to wait for them. They were walking arm in arm, and they hesitated when they saw Kurt watching them. Nevertheless, they came on, and as they approached Kurt they began making for the shoulder of the road. The brunette was rubbing her red hands. Kurt took off his glasses and smiled at them. When they were a few yards away, he asked the brunette, "Hurt?".

"It's nothing," she answered. Both girls stopped.

"Cold, huh?" Kurt tried again, with a broader smile.

As if the word had gone straight to their bones, the girls shivered. They nodded yes and headed downhill again, passing just a few inches from him. He could smell their pungent, overly sweet perfume, but just beneath it he caught the scent of a milking barn. His mother's face came to him, the feel of her lap, the fragrant warmth of her embrace and the cleft of her neck. He thought of milk and the soft sounds of the barn. In his mind he heard the song they used to sing at home about birds and winter. He whistled the first few notes under his breath and continued downhill after the girls.

The line of vehicles ended at the first curve. As they rounded the bend, a powerful gust of wind dusted snow from the boughs of the beech trees and powdered their hair and shoulders. Brushing themselves off, they caught one another's eye and laughed.

Beyond the curve, a roadside inn and a gas station appeared across the highway. Their parking lots were full of cars and trucks, but no people, except for a couple of drivers putting on chains and some traffic cops chatting with a worker from the gas station next to a snow plow.

Kurt and the girls made for the inn. Inside, the heat, smoke and noise buffeted their windburned faces. The girls moved into the room with the confidence of familiarity. They passed through the crowd at the bar and the scattered tables and went all the way to the big fireplace at the back and stood huddled before it.

Kurt hung back and went to the closest opening at the bar. He had to raise his hand half a dozen times to get the bartender's attention, and no sooner did he start to order than the man told him to speak louder. Craning his neck, Kurt could see that the girls were already eating a sandwich.

Not long after his food and beer arrived, Kurt spotted a vacant table by the door and went to sit down. He raised an arm and gestured to the girls to join him if they wanted. Customers milled about them and he couldn't see their response. He waited a couple of minutes, then decided he would have to eat alone. But just seconds later, the brunette and the blonde approached, each carrying a small cup.

Kurt swallowed, then invited them. "Sit."

The brunette lit a cigarette. The blonde took a drag off it and then gave it back. They both wrapped their hands around their hot cups. Kurt saw that their hands were red and chapped, and he felt as if his mother's and sisters' hands were touching his face and he could even smell their rough skin.

The girls sipped from their cups. Then the blonde set hers down and raised her pinkie fingernail to her teeth.

"Bad weather for travel, eh?" asked Kurt.

They nodded yes.

"I am Kurt," he told them, touching his chest.

"I'm Ana, and this is Maite," said the brunette, gesturing toward her friend.

And she added at once, "Will it take long up there?"

"How much time?" Ana rephrased, seeing Kurt's frown.

"A whole hour or more," Kurt answered, and saw anxiety darken their faces.

Maite looked at her watch, then put her lips close to Ana's ear. Kurt stared at the bar while the girls whispered.

When they finished consulting and were looking at him again, he asked, "Are you in a hurry?"

"A little bit," answered Ana.

Under the table her legs trembled, and Kurt noticed.

"Are you going to the city?" he continued.

Ana nodded yes.

"On a visit?" Kurt emphasized each syllable slightly.

Ana shook her head no. Maite lit another cigarette.

"To go shopping," said Maite.

"Shopping?" Kurt was surprised. "Bad day for shopping. Better for another day…"

Ana interrupted him. "We have to do it today, whether we want to or not."

"Ah. And to buy what?" Kurt asked, trying to smile.

Ana took a puff off Maite's cigarette and lowered her eyes before she replied, "A wreath."

Kurt kept smiling.

"Flowers," she added, "for someone who has died."

Kurt's mouth opened, then he bit his lip.

"Was it family?" he asked sadly.

"No, a friend," said Maite, to Ana's evident surprise.

They fell silent and avoided each other's eyes. Then Maite turned her head to the window. The daylight shone on her face and her strawberry-blonde hair. Within seconds they were all staring out the window.

There was nobody on the highway, uphill or down. They watched the snow squalls kicked up by the gusts of wind. Once in a while snow settled like ash on the window ledge.

Suddenly a Jeep entered their field of vision, and they drew their heads back. The vehicle was badly parked, two wheels on the highway and two in the ditch. Three women and three men got out, dressed in bright-colored ski clothes. The driver checked the ski rack on the roof. One of the men beside him bent to make a quick snowball and tossed it at the back of the nearest woman.

The three women scooped up snow to make their own and faced off against the man, who was packing another. Before long all six of them were throwing snowballs at one another, using vehicles as barricades. The game ended when one of the women was hit in the face. They all clustered around her. Her face was hidden in her hands. She recovered and the six of them walked away.

Kurt, Ana, and Maite, watched the muted scene as the six skiers vanished beyond the left edge of the window. The disappearance of the vivid colors brought them back to the bare white scene of before. They all blinked and looked at one another in disbelief.

"Ouch! Idiot!" The door of the inn opened. A woman brushed at her bottom with one hand and struck the man behind her with the other. She missed him, and the skiers laughed. As they entered, the noise inside abated for a moment. The new arrivals did not notice the hush. They went to the counter and shouted out their orders for food and drink.

Kurt swallowed the last of his beer. "I'm going to get coffee. You? Anything else?"

The girls said no. Kurt moved through the middle of the group of skiers and up to the counter. His coffee arrived and he looked over at the girls. They were deep in conversation, and Kurt wondered if he should drink his coffee at the bar. He dropped in a sugar cube, crumbled it with the little spoon, then decided to return to the table.

By the time he sat down, Ana and Maite had fallen silent. Kurt took a sip of coffee, then propped his arms on the table and leaned in closer.

"It is hard, isn't it?" He spoke abruptly, but his voice was calm and subdued. Ana looked surprised. He didn't understand why. She shook her head and raised her chin.

"What's hard?"

"Your friend."

Just as he said that, the newscaster on the inn's radio began talking about the weather and the room quieted down a bit. Some customers strained to hear. Then a second voice gave a phoned-in report on the conditions in the surrounding passes. Kurt recognized most of the place names mentioned by the announcer. "Chains," the first voice repeated. "Closed." Because of the poor radio reception, the long list of places, and the pace of the announcer's voice, Kurt didn't catch as much as he would have liked.

The news ended with the station-identification signal beeping through the inn. Some customers headed outside. Every time the door opened, a cold gust of wind hit Kurt in the back. He leaned against the wall and crossed his arms over his chest. He sneaked a glance at the girls' cheeks, still red, but now from the heat.

"What did they say?" asked Kurt, pointing a finger at the ceiling to indicate the radio.

"Chains are mandatory," said Ana.

"We knew that," said Kurt, and they all laughed.

"Don't worry," he reassured them, "you'll get there."

"I wish they would open the pass!" Maite's voice was glum.

Kurt felt another cold gust of wind. He flattened his hands on the table, a soothing gesture. "The sun is good. It will melt the snow and ice. And in the afternoon, everything will be easier." Then he added quietly, "Your friend will have those flowers."

Maite put a hand to her forehead and narrowed her eyes. "It's vital! If ours don't get there, there won't be any flowers."

Kurt looked first at one, then the other. Ana looked sideways at Maite, but she was staring out the window.

Ana began, "After living abroad for a long time…"

Kurt nodded. "Young?" he asked, his interest piqued.

"Our age," Ana answered, biting at her pinkie nail.

Maite turned slowly back to the conversation.

"Accident?" Kurt asked, lowering his voice and leaning toward them.

Ana looked confused. She seemed about to say something, then changed her mind, leaving her lips parted slightly.

Then Maite laid her left forearm on the table and tapped twice at the vein.

Kurt chewed on his lower lip and nodded to show he understood. His back was chilled again and he straightened up.

"Let me by," said Maite to Ana. "I have to go to the john."

"Wait up, I'll go with you."

The restroom was in the back of the inn, to the left of the fireplace. Kurt watched the girls as they went. Then he glanced around, blinking at his surroundings. There were half a dozen customers at the bar and another half dozen at tables.

Kurt got up and went to the counter and paid the tab for all three of them. He leaned his back against the bar and watched the comings and goings outside the window. Several vehicles started their engines and headed for the highway, including the skiers.

The girls came out of the bathroom together, deep in conversation, and kept talking for a couple of minutes next to the fireplace, leaning against the red bricks with their arms crossed and their eyes on the floor. Then they glanced at Kurt and came over to him. Without a word, the three of them made for the door.

The engine noise and exhaust outside were an incentive to stay on the porch.

"Have they actually opened it up?" asked Ana, fanning the exhaust away with a hand.

"No, I don't think so," answered Kurt. He stared at a distant point somewhere up the pass.

He was the first to move, walking slowly, not looking back. He rounded the corner on a shortcut people had made in the snow. The path led to a woodshed. His movement flushed a single dark bird. Standing in the shelter of the eaves of the woodshed, Kurt inhaled deeply the scent of split beech wood. His hands in the pockets of his jacket, he looked toward the playground a few yards down the hill. The slide and the swing-set crossbar were crusted with snow. The sun shone brightly, and the melting snow from the swing set made holes in the white crust on the ground. Kurt heard a bird caw from the ravine and the sound of more water. A gust of wind carried a wisp of smoke that dissipated in the morning air. He smelled burning beech wood.

Kurt looked back toward the inn and saw the girls a few yards away, standing silently, staring at the playground. Kurt watched them until they returned his gaze.

"Let's go slow," he said, lifting his chin and smiling at them.

The girls blinked at him. When he reached their side, they started off, holding on to one another and watching the ground to keep from slipping in the grimy slush. Kurt noticed that the girls were wearing dress shoes. Their toes were soaked and their stockings were splashed with mud.

They wove their way through the idling cars and stepped out on the highway. Silently, they headed uphill.

People were standing by their vehicles now, talking and horsing around in the snow. Only a few were sitting inside with the engines running. Snatches of sound from a newscast or a radio show drifted on the air. As they neared the flat meadow, they could feel the north wind more strongly.

When they reached the girls' car, Kurt stopped and pointed at his truck.

"That's mine."

The girls seemed not to have heard him. Then after a second or so, Ana said, "See you." She took out her keys and she and Maite got in the car.

Kurt watched as Ana started the engine.

When he reached the cab of his truck, he could see that the road was almost cleared, but the bright yellow crane was still working to remove the wreck.

He climbed into his cab and started the engine. The interior warmed up quickly and made him sleepy. He thought about the dreary hours he'd spent at the bottom of the hill the night before. He rubbed his eyes, turned off the engine, and half-opened a window. The meadow was on his left, and a hundred yards away three skiers were moving by fits and starts along on the flat.

It was ten-twenty by the dashboard clock. Kurt remembered that he was supposed to call home that night. He shut the window and folded his arms. He began singing a sad song.

Two figures jogged by up the center of the highway. A couple of minutes later, the truck in front of Kurt started its engine, and after another pause, it began to move slowly, inch by inch for the first third of a mile.

Once they reached the other side of the watershed, the going was easier. Near the summit, where the beech groves began in earnest, were two Jeeps. In red berets, their drivers were standing on the shoulder of the road, watching the vehicles stream by. A few yards farther on was the opposite line of traffic, waiting for the police to give the order to move. As Kurt moved downhill, he caught glimpses of the faces of the drivers in the other lane, and he fancied he could see their exhaustion. All the way down the hill, he glanced at the rearview mirror and each time he could see the girls' white car.

Then he remembered the border crossing up ahead and brought his attention back to the highway.

After the second tunnel, traffic began to slow. The first two jams didn't last long and he wasn't worried. But during the third jam, Kurt realized they were near a bridge he'd crossed many times. He knew what tended to happen there. They inched along for two hundred yards, almost up to the bridge. Then the ambulance arrived and they had to sit and wait.

A piece of tailgate from a big rig lay in the highway. It must have hit the pylon.

Kurt was sitting at the beginning of a curve and had a broad field of vision. His eyes darted again to the rearview mirror, looking for the girls' car. They were still behind him. He turned off the motor and opened his window. He leaned his elbow out the window and breathed deeply of the fresh air. It wasn't nearly as cold now.

After a bit, the sound of a metal saw drowned out the muted buzz of surrounding engines. For several minutes, the air was filled with the noise from the power saw and the shouting of workers giving orders. Kurt closed his window. Then he folded his arms, rested his neck on the back of the seat and tried to sleep. The outside noise

was muted with the window up. He imagined sparks
flying off the metal.

He opened his eyes at the sound of the ambulance
siren. From the inside someone closed its back door.
Another person got in beside the driver, and they took
off with lights flashing and siren blaring.

After a while, the road was cleared. As they continued downhill, the traffic jam eased, and as soon as they
hit snowless stretches of road, vehicles began passing each
other.

After the first town, the girls' car passed Kurt's truck.
As it moved up alongside him, it seemed to Kurt that
they gave him a little nod of farewell, like fellow travelers
in the wilderness.

Kurt let his eyes stray to the mountains sleek with
snow. Beyond that sea of white would lie the sea of blue,
and the border, and songs and birds, and with the music
the white bouquet of the cold.

XABIER MONTOIA (Gasteiz)

When I was a kid, we were the only ones on the block without a TV set. Of course, my brother and I both hated it – not only were we the laughing stock of the other children, but our only entertainment was just the radio and a few books my dad had. I guess that was when I began to dream, first about being a musician, and later about being a writer. Childish dreams, no doubt, but dreams that have kept me alive ever since. So far I have nine LPs, several singles, three books of poetry, three novels and three collections of short stories: *Emakume biboteduna* (1992, *The Mustachioed Woman*), *Gasteizko hondartzak* (1997, *The Beaches of Gasteiz*) and *Baina bihotzak dio* (2002, *But the Heart Says*). My dreams have come true, but dreams don't pay the rent. So I wake up every morning and go to work for, of all things, a TV station, or as Bernardo Atxaga (the best known and best paid Basque author ever) once reproached me, "at the heart of the state." That's my life. The rest is silence.

Black As Coal

by

XABIER MONTOIA

Translated by Kristin Addis

Probably the only thing we all have in common is the one day we never forget: the sweet memory of the first time we quench the body's fire in another. (I had sex for the first time on April 27, 1937). I would bet that no one forgets; it's etched in the brain, like rust on iron. This damned memory, tougher than steel. (The skies were clear over Gernika).

There's a time in every man's life when he stops being a child and even though he's not yet a man and doesn't yet know the path his life will take, he sets off in the race whose only finish line is death. (Those were difficult years for me, and not only because of the war). We learn that later, of course, much later, and until we figure it out, we race like madmen, always trying to get ahead, eager to reach the paradise of adulthood. And in this race, as if we were cars, our main fuel is sex; it pushes us on, spurs and goads us. (I thought I was sick, laid low by an illness that only I suffered). At that age of doubts, we are drenched by the saturating flow whose milky liquid pervades everything.

Without the slightest success I tried to think about anything else, but there was nothing at all that didn't bring sex to mind one way or another. Had I been blind-

ed by a branding iron, I would have kept right on seeing
reminders of sex everywhere. Even blind, the wind would
bring me its smells and sounds. I would have to die to be
free of this malady.

At first I thought I was the only sick one. But later I
learned that Teo and I suffered the same illness. The same
illness I say, but it would be more accurate to say a similar illness, because although Teo felt the same urgency in
his groin, at least he had someone to talk to. We would
meet in a corner of the kitchen and he would tell me the
ups and downs of his experiences with girls at the previous Sunday's dance at the Florida. I, on the other hand,
had to keep everything to myself. (And the afflictions of
love and of the body worsen if you can't let them out.
Just like with wine — the best wine in the world turns to
vinegar if kept in the bottle long enough). I knew I
would lose my friend if ever I mentioned the fire that
burned inside me. And not only that; the way things
were then, I could also lose my job if the faintest rumors
of my feelings reached the hotel. And they would, without a doubt.

We had one afternoon a week free, sometimes Sunday, often Monday. If we happened to get a Sunday, we
went dancing. The Hotel Fronton workers were allowed
to go free to the dances held at the jai alai court once the
games were over for the day. But we preferred the dances
at the Florida. To tell the truth, I didn't care one way or
the other since either way, I wouldn't move from my spot
by the orchestra. Teo on the other hand, met a lot of girls
in the park whose only shelter was the open sky. We were
poor and so were our friends.

Teo tried to introduce me to the girls he knew. And
gave up fast:

"You're hopeless!"

Evidently my good-hearted friend didn't realize that my eyes weren't drawn to these girls he admired so much, but to the stocky young workers who grabbed them boldly around the waist; he didn't notice that my attention wasn't on these girls who stuffed their bras with pages of old newspapers, but on the boys fighting to the death to dance with them, strong and muscular, sweaty.

Teo stayed until the orchestra in the bandstand played the last song. I left earlier, claiming to be tired, taking the Senda walkway with the beat of the tango softer and softer behind me. I found peace there, as if the sturdy trees that lined the path were watching over me. In that darkness, I felt something akin to freedom. Finally I would give in to tears, the miserable and anguished tears that burned my cheeks yet also brought a certain calm. And when I reached the iron bridge, the bridge where I had once seen a man hanging from a rope around his neck, I would stop beneath it; I could see myself hanging there then, ending my pain and torment and doubts forever with one simple act.

Death was my only way out. And if I didn't do it, it was only because another stronger force was holding me back: the desires of the flesh. Torn between one thing and the other, my heart was breaking. If I had to die to the soft beat of the melody floating on the wind, I wanted to see my death reflected in the gypsy eyes of the dancing boys. How could I leave this world without fulfilling the dream that woke me every night? How could I leave without knowing it at least once? And even without dying, I spent long periods of time apart from the world, strangled by my worries, unable to bear the passage of time. The rattle of the train brought me back among the living. The sudden noise startled me, exploding unexpectedly over my head and, not remembering where I was, I took the noise of the train for a gunshot. And I don't know why, because ever since the war started not a single shot had been heard in Gasteiz.

Or more precisely, one shot was heard: on San Prudencio street, in the festivities they organized with the arms they had confiscated from the Reds, a sergeant, allegedly drunk, mounted a small tank and fired off a round. But I didn't hear it. I was asleep and didn't know anything about it until I arrived at work the next day.

"That was a close one!"

It was all people could talk about. They came to the hotel and stood looking up toward the place where the ill-fated round had entered. It had gone through a wall and blown up in a first-floor room, number 108, one I had often cleaned. Thank God it was empty that night.

The things I like have always been essentially the same. Most of the things I love, I first discovered when I was young: music, alcohol, the cinema, cars… and sex; our distractions from an empty and wretched life. The cinema must have been the first thing that seduced me. If our weekly afternoon off didn't fall on a Sunday, we would spend it in the Principe Theater next to the hotel, devouring the Fox newsreel and two films together with the sandwiches smuggled out to us by Luis who worked in the kitchen. We didn't care much what was showing, we loved everything the same: Fred Astaire and Ginger Rogers, Mickey Mouse, or films from the German company UFA.

And so my life went on. On the one hand, wanting to deny my nature but once and again caught up in the intense and unmentionable conflict of my desires. And on the other hand, running from my wicked obsession and finding refuge in the darkness of the theater.

With all this, I hardly noticed any change with the coming of the war. Maybe because I was living in a virtual world, one in which I was the only inhabitant other than Hollywood stars. In any case, few changes were evident even in the so-called real world. Not even the war itself could split apart the ordinary life of the little town where I was born on that unfortunate day. For the people walking up and down Dato Street, everything continued the same, at least superficially. Also for those who gathered in the afternoon for tea at the hotel; they still came without fail. The only difference about them was their clothes: they left their felt caps at home and started wearing red berets as soon as the war started. Most of them wore gray shirts, some wore blue; they all marched around proudly in shiny black leather boots and belts.

They chattered in front of me, sifting through all the news from the front, angry with the brutality of the Reds, repeating the sacrileges, the black sins they were said to commit, cursing the European democracies.

"If it weren't for the help of those sons of bitches…!"

I always agreed, though my mind was full of my own war. Now that was a war, a real one. Not the one they waged with a coffee cup in one hand, a fat Havana cigar in the other. I was the one forever bleeding, forever dying. But my trenches, my battlefield, though not at Legutio or Otxandio, weren't far from our brave soldiers, waiter bring this, waiter carry that, with no respite.

I was literally under their very feet. The kitchen was beneath the tearoom, and further on, beyond a dark patio, the coal room. My first duty was to light the ovens for the kitchen and the boiler for the hotel. When I was seized by my madness, by my urgent need for sexual release, I hid myself between the piles of coal destined for the ovens and the boiler and, as soon as I had dropped my pants, spilled my pearly drops over the black coal. Straightening up again, I would be almost dizzy for a while, spent. Then I would take my handkerchief out of my pocket with my left hand and wipe off the right with it, as fast as possible. Taking the shovel in my freshly wiped hands, I would try to cover up all traces of my sticky seed. I crossed the patio with my head down, moving fast in my fear even though I knew there couldn't have been any witnesses to my indecent act. I would calm down once I reached the kitchen.

Nevertheless, all that was only the prelude to the war. When the Germans arrived at the Hotel Fronton, that's when the real war started for me, the one that would permeate every aspect of my life.

I hardly noticed Hans at first. He was neither short nor ugly, but since all of those pilots were young and most were handsome, he didn't stand out right away. He was tall, slender. Because of this, he was almost invisible among his companions. Or you could say he disappeared behind the curtain of so many green uniforms.

I liked these Germans. Accustomed to our local boastful Red Berets, I was surprised at the Germans' behavior. They said please whenever they asked for anything and, once they had it, never failed to say thank you. They were so different from the arrogant Falangists or the Italians who spent all day perfuming themselves and preening their mustaches. By then I had seen all types of uniforms. For one born in the country but forced to move to Gasteiz at six months, and raised then in this city abounding with military men and priests, the sight of uniforms was part of the everyday landscape. And yet, these uniforms were alluring. The uniforms or the uniformed? It didn't matter. In the state I was in, I would have been ecstatic to go with the shabbiest of them, grateful for caresses from even the dirtiest hand. How could I not fret then, at the side of these strapping happy blond boys!

Hans, however, had dark hair. His eyes, instead of being the blue of the clear sky, were the gray of the sea before a storm. I saw him for the first time on a Saturday night. Called to room 211, I knocked on the door and he opened it for me. He stood before me in a military jacket with the top buttons undone, barefoot, a drinking glass in one hand.

"Ice, please," he said in Spanish, dragging out each syllable.

The notes of a pasodoble floated up from the ballroom, an invitation to dance.

From then on it happened that I would often be called to serve that room. He would invite me in and, after leaving whatever he had asked for on the desk by the window, he would thank me with a wide smile. Sometimes he gave me cigarettes too, strong tobacco from Germany.

And one of those times, once when I had finished my work and he had offered me a cigarette in thanks, I started to put it in my pocket, but he lit a match and came over next to me. I looked into the flame for a second. I could feel the heat on the end of my nose. My attention was drawn to his face. It seemed to me to be more intense than usual. I raised the cigarette to my lips and bent slightly toward the flame, toward his hand. The first mouthful of smoke ripped into my lungs like a pitchfork and I broke out coughing. How embarrassing. But the more I tried to hold in the damned cough, the louder and stronger it became. Hans said something I didn't understand. He started to pound me on the back, trying to ease my cough. When I finally managed to catch my breath, my eyes were full of tears. I didn't need to see anything anyway, didn't want to see anything. It was enough to feel his hand moving softly from my back to my neck, from my neck to my head.

That's how it all started.

Or just barely started, since Hans wasn't in any sort of hurry. I was. What I had heard so many times as an insult now became a gentle refrain in my imagination. But he wanted to keep me waiting. Maybe I seemed too fragile to him. I don't know, maybe he was afraid that I would break into a million pieces in his hands. And just in case, he went slowly with me.

Days passed before I could finally fulfill my desire. Even if the date didn't appear in every history text, I could never forget it since the day before had been the anniversary of Iñaki's death; in what had surely been Gasteiz's very first traffic accident, my older brother had been hit by a car a year earlier.

The pilots had returned jubilantly to the hotel that afternoon. Instead of going to their rooms as usual, they went straight to the bar. We heard loud guffaws, the sounds of glasses clinking and songs.

"What are they celebrating?" asked Teo.

"I don't know. Whatever it is, it must be important! Listen to how happy they are!"

Hans was the first to leave the bar. On the way to his room, he stopped before the elevator and smiled at me.

Soon he called down and I raced up the stairs. He opened the door as soon as I knocked. I smelled the sharp scent of alcohol on his breath, in that mouth where I wanted to slake the thirst I had endured so long. I went in and, hardly giving me time to set down the beer I had brought up to him, he started to undo the buttons on my jacket.

When I got up from Hans' bed, I gathered up my pants which had fallen to the floor and tried to smooth out the wrinkles with my hand. Then, in a notebook open on the desk, I recognized a word I had never given much importance to before: Gernika; the only word I could make out among all the German words around it. Gernika, a name I had once heard from my mother, but one which meant nothing to one who walked rather than flew. I flew out of Hans' room, with the lightness that is one of the few gifts of love.

We were together for two happy months. But we both knew that the walls of Hans' room with their flowered wallpaper marked the boundaries of our love. Outside of that room, we were nothing.

I wanted to tell the world of my happiness. Especially Teo, since he had quickly noticed the change in me. And dying of curiosity, he never tired of asking.

"What's her name?"

"OK, Teo, that's enough…"

"Come on, tell me her name!"

"Ana," I lied, using the name of some silly girl from our neighborhood.

"You have to introduce me! If she can make you that crazy, I've got to meet her!"

"Yeah, Teo, OK, next week." Another lie.

If anyone had found out what was happening in room 211, I would have been in great danger. In times of war people's normal meanness is that much stronger. If love between two men is looked down upon today, imagine how much worse it was in the atmosphere of war. On the street, I would ditch Teo as fast as possible to return to the hotel, to breach the borders and enter the small gift box of our love, wrapped in flowered paper. In silence we satisfied the feverish needs of our two young bodies and the desires that burned inside us and had to be kept secret, never to be let out.

Hans was homesick and often spoke of his homeland and about everything he had left behind. It must have been beautiful: an enormous cathedral, palaces, long avenues, lavish gardens. I could see it all shining in his stormy eyes. And I dreamed I would see it all with him, my mind dancing with the exotic names but mute, knowing I could offer nothing to compare with such marvelous things. What did I have to talk about? About my job at the hotel? About our cramped house, barely big enough for my parents and brothers and sisters? What could one say who had never been out of little Gasteiz after hearing such wondrous tales of Cologne?

And then, when he talked about the Spaniards, his smile would twist and his face would darken.

"We'll never win the war that way!" he would complain, unable to erase the latest idiocy of a fascist general from his mind. "There's no discipline in this army. The officers are nothing but a big bunch of arrogant morons, and the soldiers are all brawn and no brains. They have no ideals or anything, only their own hunger."

He had no respect for anybody, not even for those who were paying for the Germans to be there. He got furious every time he heard the name Oriol, and his tongue sharpened with insults. These words frightened me. The walls had ears in those times. The mere mention of Oriol's name was enough to bring him to mind, a massive man who never removed his red beret for anything or anyone. Oriol was as sturdy as a mast, like his sons and daughters. I remember him well, even now after almost seventy years. His sons wore the red beret like their father, his daughters dressed in nurses' whites.

"They're all short and swarthy, like gypsies. That's what they are: gypsies!"

I agreed with his opinion of the citizens of Gasteiz without realizing that I also numbered among them. I've always been short and dark, unlearned. There wasn't much difference between me and those who filled the streets, bars, and hospitals. When we're young, however, we only want to see what makes us different from everyone else. It's only with age that we begin to see the strong but almost imperceptible ties that bind us to our birthplace. They are our roots and, even hidden underground, they hold the tree steady. And just like the roots of a tree, I had to stay underground; I had to hide all my yearnings, dreams, desires, and thoughts. The need for secrecy forced me away from others and my loneliness was greater than ever.

How could I think, how could it even occur to me, that these contemptuous words spoken by the man I loved applied to me as well? He never told me any such thing. He always behaved courteously with me. What was I to him? Just another insignificant Spaniard, another *untermann* just barely good enough to take it up the ass. And even so, I was all too happy to accept the kisses and poison he gave me.

It's so hard to find out that someone you loved so much was a mercenary, an assassin. I have often asked myself what I would have done if I had known what lay behind the word Gernika which I had read by chance in Hans' notebook. (The skies were clear over Gernika). I know the answer: I would have loved him just the same, I would have made excuses for him. Even now, even though I know what happened there in all its rawness, I am unable to change the sweet memory of my young pilot. Massacres are scummy foamy waters racing downstream. The currents of our daily small betrayals and large disappointments would carry us away but for these crumbs of pleasant memory — our branches, which we grab onto with wounded hands, hoping to be saved.

At the time I didn't know these disturbing things, fortunately.

I would go out at night and, leaving the exhaustion of my full day's work at the hotel door, I would start looking forward to the next day. And when I couldn't be with Hans, instead of going straight home, I would take the detour down the Senda. All the tears I had shed in the shade of its trees had become smiles of elation as soon as I met the German pilot. And I kept going back then also to my favorite place in the city, the place where earlier I had sought peace in my bitterest moments.

Will he call for me tomorrow? I whispered to myself in the dark. Oh, my beloved Hans!

Though the morning was cool, the day would be warm. The day before, it had rained without stopping and the change was welcome. Thursday dawned clear and Thursdays were Pola Negri days. Mr. Alti, the owner of the Hotel Fronton, had a car we had dubbed Pola

Negri. The real Pola Negri was a movie actress who was very famous at the time. Pola Negri was not black, and it was only because of her last name that we had named the boss' Citroën after her. It was as black as the coal on the far side of the patio, except for the elegant white lines that ran on either side of the car from nose to tail. Again and again I polished those lines with a rag until I left the car shining. But I enjoyed this job: by then I had become aware of the similarities between the bodies of cars and men, and I found the harmony of Hans' body in the Citroën. Caressing the fin that started behind the door and grew into the fender, I could imagine that I was stroking my beloved's rugged arms, that I could sense his firm muscles and proud bearing, that I felt the same tingle in my fingertips as when I touched him.

I was pondering this when the bells of Saint Michael's sounded eight o'clock.

When I raised my eyes to the clock tower I saw it. It came down in a trail of smoke: a Heinkel 51, the kind Hans flew. I took off running for the Plaza Berri, where the airplane was going to crash.

It happened so quickly. The Heinkel hit the kiosk in the middle of the plaza, caught fire and blew up in the corner. I didn't see any more.

"Don't move!" I heard the voice of the man who had thrown me to the ground.

It was a policeman. I owe him my life. If he hadn't thrust me behind a pillar of the arcade, I would have died in the inferno of the explosion: the whine of munitions, broken glass from the shop windows, shrapnel, ashes, and smoke. I couldn't catch my breath. The policeman's face was bloody and I could feel blood on my own cheeks as well. I panicked then, worried about the pilot.

"Hans!" The terrified cry leapt out of me.

I wanted to go over to the burning Heinkel, but the policeman's arms held me back.

"Let me go!" I cried.

"Stay put, boy!" He wouldn't turn me loose. "Don't budge, dammit!"

They took me to the hospital. I only had a few scrapes and I broke away from them, limping.

"Where were you? Are you OK?" Teo hugged me at the entrance to the hotel. "Were you in the plaza?"

I couldn't answer. The question was burning on my tongue but I held it in, afraid to give away my relationship with Hans.

"It was the guy in 211," Teo whispered in my ear as if he knew what I was thinking.

I didn't cry. My knees were shaking and I would have fallen had Teo not held me up. No moan fell from my lips. Hans and I were bound together, and I had to keep our secret no matter what. My pain didn't betray me.

"Let's go to the room," was all Teo said to me.

"No!" I understood him at once.

But we got in the elevator anyway. Teo took me to Hans' room. Those were tough times and there might be something worth taking home; we couldn't afford to pass up this rare opportunity. The room was open. We closed the door behind us and, without speaking, set to looking for things to appropriate. I already knew there wasn't much of any value.

"Look at these cigarettes," Teo had made a find.

I took advantage of his distraction to hide some photos from a desk drawer under my jacket. We divided the cigarettes in the coal room and Teo smoked one.

Leaving the hotel, I went home by way of the Senda that evening as well. Arriving at the iron bridge, the hanged man I had seen long ago appeared again before my eyes. And the same thing happened the next day. And the next. Death was calling me and its song was sweet.

On the third day after Hans died, the head chef gave me some parcels wrapped up in newspaper. I had to take them to the airfield. There was a taxi waiting for me outside. It was drizzling. There were two landing strips in Gasteiz then: one at Lakua for the small airplanes, and the other by Judizmendi, where I told the taxi driver to take me.

On the tarmac, a single airplane was swimming in the thin rain, motor roaring. I passed the parcels up to the pilot: food for a long journey, apparently. The plane seemed smaller from the inside than from outside. It was dark inside, but right away I made out a black coffin, gold letters on the lid. Without reading it, I knew whose it was. I dissolved in tears.

That was how Hans' comrades found me. Hans Schwarz's death was not in vain, nor was it absurd; my own sobs were proof of that. The war was not in vain, nor was it absurd, since good people were in favor of it.

"Once we free the country of communism, we'll need men like you," an officer told me.

And the taxi driver said almost the same thing when I returned red-eyed to the car.

We know that when elephants feel death approaching, they set out for their ancestors' graveyard. Though they've never been there before, they find that merciful route. That's what came to my mind this morning. I went to the plaza, thinking to see again the scar left on the wall by the explosion of Hans' plane. I couldn't say what compelled me to go.

Am I not myself an old and weary elephant?

I didn't find anything new. The scars had been there for years. I remember how, after the war ended, the cracks in the wall persisted and the blackened stones remained. But everything changes. They took the kiosk out of the middle of the plaza. What was once the Plaza Berri became the Plaza España overnight. Yes, things change a lot it seems. But if you scratch the surface a little, the opacity falls away and you can see things again as they used to be. These images have been with me ever since I returned to Gasteiz. Even though they have opened things up and modernized things since I left, nothing essential has changed. The people who forced me to leave the city must still be there, or their descendants, as wicked as they and as evil. They carry these wrongs in their blood. And that can't be changed. It would take centuries, or the fire that incinerated Han's Heinkel. Who knows?

This morning, when I was looking for traces on the plaza walls, another morning came to mind, a clear-skied Thursday morning of long ago. Pulling on the thread of these memories that weigh so heavily on me, my hand found the inner pocket of my jacket, seeking the photo I had kept since then. It has yellowed with time. Standing between a man and a woman, a small child with gray stormy eyes, a shy smile on his lips: Hans Schwarz, the one I loved the best.

On the last day of the war, I learned that the German word schwarz means black.

INAZIO MUJIKA IRAOLA (Donostia, 1963)

I was born in Donostia in 1963, four days before somebody shot President Kennedy. So it wasn't me. I completed my Teacher's Certificate and got my degree in Basque philology. For the most part, I have written short stories. Some have appeared in my books; others have not. My first collection came out in 1987: *Azukrea belazeetan* (*Sugar on the Prairie*). This strange title is a metaphor for snow, and snow itself is a metaphor for my first homeland: childhood. My story *Linkon* (1991), published as part of a series for children, didn't appear in this collection though now I think perhaps it belongs there. I am so fond of legends that those that exist seem too few and I made up new ones for my book *Hautsaren kronika* (*Chronicle of Dust*), published in 1994. War has always seemed to me to be the perfect theater for examining the light and darkness of human character. Any war will do, but since it was most familiar to me, I began to write fiction about the Spanish Civil

War and the period of the German occupation of France. My first offering was the story that appears here, *Itoak ur azalera bezala* (1992, *Like the waters release their dead*), which I had intended to be the seed of a larger collection. The same was true of my short book *Matriuska* (1995), which is comprised of only three stories. My last book to date is *Gerezi denbora* (1999, *Cherry Season*); they say it's a novel, but I consider it a long story. I turned in the proofs of this book to the publisher one day, and that night my twins were born, a boy and a girl; a good harvest for the season so to speak. You will certainly understand why I haven't written more since then.

I work as an editor. In 1993, I founded the publishing house Alberdania with my friend Jorge Gimenez. I am also a scriptwriter, and I wrote the script for the cartoon film *Karramarro Uhartea* (2000, *Crab Island*, Goya prize winner) with Joxean Muñoz. I've done other things as well, but I won't mention everything here.

Like The Waters Release Their Dead

by

INAZIO MUJIKA IRAOLA

Translated by Kristin Addis

I arrived at Austerlitz at dusk and, unable to drive the summer stench from my nostrils, headed into the city walking along the left bank of the Seine. I took the Boulevard Saint-Michel up to the Latin Quarter, setting my bags on the ground from time to time to give my hands a rest and let go of the handles for a bit before setting out along the river again. I had the address written on a piece of paper and I saw the blue sign on a wall, Rue Mouffetard. That was it. I checked the number and without further ado, rang the bell at the boarding house. A woman about my age opened the door for me, turning the deadbolt three or four times. I asked if there were rooms available. She told me to enter and made me sit in the entrance, pushing me into my seat with her hand on my shoulder. I waited for her there while she went somewhere looking for the registration forms.

There were cats milling around on the chairs and tabletops. They were old cats, many of them mangy. Black cats, cats that had once been black, calico cats, butterscotch cats. I counted about half a dozen. They approached my chair, but were spooked away as soon as I made the slightest gesture. There was a display case by

the window, and inside, stuffed cats in a variety of pos-
tures, there forever, trapped and staring.

The woman returned with a scrap of old paper in her
hands, but left me again to find a pen. Finally I started
on the paperwork. The form hadn't been updated in
years from what I could see, since the space for the date
was marked 194_. I crossed off the four and wrote in a six
on the yellowed page and, following that, a one.

We agreed on the price right away, and the woman
picked up a key and took me to my room. She opened
the door and I saw the furniture. It was old of course, but
I was surprised to see that it was covered with newspapers. All except a rocking chair next to the bay window.
The woman went in ahead of me and immediately started to remove the newspapers very carefully from the furniture. I told her I would do that myself. She ignored me.
I raised my voice and told her to quit it, I wanted to be
alone to relax, I had had a long journey. She didn't stop,
however, until she had removed all the papers. She gathered them up and placed them on the small bottom shelf
of the wardrobe without wrinkling or folding a single
page.

I lay down on the bed. I was amazed that the woman
hadn't read me the rules of the house, line by line, as was
customary in other boarding houses, and I was grateful.
Everything in the room was arranged around the bed, a
double, with a night table next to it and an old lamp with
a well-used and bent lampshade. Above the bed was a
cross, and on the left-hand wall, obscured by dust and its
own black paint, a gypsy's face stared out of a picture. On
the same wall, a sort of bay window and, in front of it,
the rocking chair. A wardrobe for my clothes, a desk, and
a straight chair.

My company had sent me first to Lyon, then to Paris, to visit our branch offices and write a report in which, with an eye to the future, I was to suggest any changes that would be worth implementing at home, *clearly and completely*, as my boss had repeated several times. Since I had much to report on my Lyon experience, many notes and such, I had to start organizing my thoughts, so I asked the woman if the sound of my typewriter might bother her, but she told me to go ahead and not to worry about it.

I didn't eat dinner. On the train I had had a sandwich and a Coke, and the cold drink or the gummy bread, one or the other, wasn't sitting right with me. The next day, I got up early, and found that the reception room with the stuffed cats had become the breakfast room. There were four bowls laid out in a row and two men eating breakfast sitting on tall-backed chairs. The woman greeted me politely, and pointed out my bowl. As soon as I sat down, she picked up a yellow card from in front of my bowl on which the number 6 had been drawn. The number of my room. Beside me I had a one-armed bald man. He must have lost his arm quite a while ago I thought, since he handled his silverware with ease. Before five minutes had passed, he introduced himself. "*Gérard. Ancien combattant.*" I smiled vaguely at him, but he didn't seem to understand my smile. "*Et vous?*"

I said I was a traveling salesman, thinking that would be enough. But before breakfast was over, I was obliged to give more details. I don't remember now what I said. I fed him one lie after another, as fast as I could cook them up.

I left the boarding house and decided I would spend the day walking around, on the pretext of having to buy paper. I didn't have to visit the company until the next day. I ate lunch out as well and, after having a mint tea, I returned to the boarding house, my clean white pages under my arm. I started to work and spent an hour on a single blank page, trying unsuccessfully to figure out how to begin the report that would contain all the details on Lyon. I had started writing when the woman suddenly entered the room, carrying a drinking glass full of water in her left hand and a black bag in her right hand. She didn't say anything except to excuse herself. She sat down in the armchair, turning sideways to the light slanting in.

"Keep working and don't mind me," she said when she realized I had stopped and was staring at her. She set the glass on the windowsill, took out her false teeth and dropped them in. Although until then I had been staring at her, now, embarrassed for her, I looked down at my page.

"I'm more comfortable like this."

She took out her glasses then from her black bag, and taking out a skein of yarn and knitting needles from a plastic pouch, began to knit, completely at ease.

"This is my little corner."

I stared at her in disbelief, but didn't have the nerve to throw her out. Finally, unable to forget she was there, I resigned myself to her presence and went back to my report. I kept looking at her out of the corner of my eye, sitting there knitting in the rocking chair. She didn't say a word. She just knit. I started to write something though I was completely distracted and couldn't concentrate on what I was doing.

An hour passed and she left as she had come, gathering everything up and saying "see you tomorrow."

To tell the truth, my agitation was more than just a passing irritation. The next day if she came, I would tell her once and for all that she couldn't be there and, if she refused, I would change rooms or leave the boarding house altogether. But she came the next day, appearing before me at the same time as the day before, saying "back to my little corner," knitting materials in one hand and glass for her false teeth in the other. The same thing happened the next day as well, and still I couldn't get up the nerve to say anything. She sat in my room as the clock in the hall struck four and stayed until she heard the five o'clock bells. Finally I became accustomed to working in her presence. I worked on my report, she worked on her sweater, dark blue. Sometimes she worked on men's undergarments or darned the heels of socks.

In that same week and while the woman was there, one of the cats came into my room. It walked around and around from one side to the other, inspecting the room and all the furniture. Even insurance inspectors don't examine things so closely, I thought. The cat came all the way over near my leg and tentatively passed its tail over my shoes. Finally, when I didn't yell at it or frighten it away, it began to play at my feet. Tiring, it stretched out under the table, then woke up again and jumped up onto my desk. At this, I did start to object. But the woman got in ahead of me. "Kitty!" she called. "Can't you see you're bothering the man?" The cat jumped down and slunk through the door. "He's very playful," she said, shaking her head with a superficial smile. "*Je suis désolée.*"

From the bathroom window you could see an uncovered interior patio with a single tree and a few small weeds between the paving stones. In the twilight at dusk, I would see the woman on the patio gathering all the cats around her and tossing food to them, offering bread, soggy bread, no doubt moistened with milk.

I kept writing my report and the woman kept knitting away at her sweater. When she finished the back, she asked me to please stand up so she could check the size. I rose and went to stand before her. She held the blue back of the sweater up to my back, holding her knitting needles between her lips. "*Je suis désolée*," she said, she had made it too big. She started unraveling it. I asked her who it was for but she didn't answer. "*Chui désolée, chui désolée*" was all she said, "I have to do it over."

If Kitty came to the door, the woman would say "scat" angrily. "It's unbelievable, Kitty, how stubborn you are. You still haven't learned to do what I say. I already told you you're bothering the man." Then she looked at me, saying "sorry, mister" over and over, smiling her eerie toothless smile.

At the breakfast table the former soldier had told me of a thousand battles by this time and, tiring of his own stories, now asked me if we hadn't also had a war in Spain and what I had done in it. I started telling him about my tough times in jail. The dismal lights in the hallways at night, the sound of the wardens' steps in the corridors, silence and gunshots in the morning. The old man followed my bloody stories avidly. I had heard them all from my brother, to whom they had really happened, but I told them as if they were my own, with all the details, though hiding, of course, that I had been among the winners in the Spanish Civil War, had even become a second lieutenant.

Out of solidarity or something, since we were trading stories, he seemed to think he had to say something and he told me he was a taxidermist, he stuffed cats. He had stuffed the ones in the display case. He had learned the art in the concentration camp, where the Nazis had done it to the Jews, testing taxidermy on humans. Since he also knew German, he had made himself useful as a doctor's assistant and had seen what went on there. *"C'est la guerre,"* he told me.

I took advantage of the old man's chattiness to ask about the boarding house woman. Without much interest, he told me about her late husband; he had been a member of the brigades in the Spanish Civil War and had been killed there. The woman was already quite unbalanced by the time the old man had met her; she had been denounced as a Nazi collaborator after the liberation of Paris.

I kept working on my report, going to the company in the morning to gather my data, eating lunch out, then returning home to the usual visit from four to five. One of those days, when I'd been there for twenty days or so, the woman missed her daily visit and the cat startled me, jumping in through the bay window. My heart pounded. Once I had calmed down, I coaxed it over to me saying "here puss, puss, puss," even though it didn't seem very interested at first.

I passed the palm of my hand over the cat from head to tail but when I least expected it, it scratched me on the hand. Three red lines. Blinded by sudden hatred, I grabbed it by the neck, squeezing and squeezing, I would make it afraid of me. It scratched and yowled, but finally lay dead in my hands.

I left the lifeless black form on the chair and, looking at myself in the mirror, realized I was all bloody. Another three red lines on my face. I cleaned myself up quickly and, after rubbing my wounds with alcohol, looked out the bathroom window, half hiding myself behind the curtain. There was the woman feeding the cats. I didn't know what to tell her about the cat, and I left it lying in the hallway, hoping she would bring it up. I thought up a thousand excuses. I stood tensely behind my door, waiting for the woman to return. When she opened the door I heard footsteps, and suddenly:

"Oh, Kitty! I told you, Kitty, not to bother the man. I told you and told you and you didn't listen."

That evening I didn't leave my room.

The woman, on the other hand, never said a word to me about it, neither at breakfast the next morning nor at any time after that.

She never again missed her four o'clock appointment in my room. Having finished the back of the sweater, she now started on the sides. She finished the sides, and then did the sleeves. Whenever I sat down at the typewriter, a thousand questions would come to mind.

Out of the blue, I was seized by a strong desire to know what had really happened to her husband and I somehow found the nerve to ask. She answered as politely as ever that her husband had been killed in the war, the Spanish Civil War, and she described him to me with a nostalgic smile. He had been a volunteer in the international brigades, and she had a photograph of him that she would show me. She put in her false teeth and left the room. In five minutes she was back with the picture. Again my heart pounded involuntarily. The picture had yellowed. There was a grove of trees in the background, and two men bathing their feet in a creek, one dressed as a soldier and the other with a camera, sleeves rolled up and sitting on his jacket. I was the soldier. The long-closed corners of my brain snapped open, releasing their half-buried memories.

Like the waters eventually release their dead.

Marcel had introduced himself to us as a journalist in the convent at Teruel which we had seized before the one at Ebro. I myself was a second lieutenant and had command of a company in the absence of a lieutenant. Our superior officers had left me in charge of this man; because I knew French, they said I could show him what kind of soldiers Franco had and he could tell the world.

Marcel seemed to be a good person to confide in, and we became fast friends. Over a period of months, even if you don't come to know a person well, you still learn many reliable facts about him, even in difficult times. We talked for long hours about things we had read and, before going to bed, about when we hoped to go to the front.

But once when I was on guard duty, the sentry came to me because he had seen lights in the colonel's office. We went there and when we opened the door, we found the window wide open and a shadow making a hasty escape. We ran after him and finally caught him. It was Marcel. If I had been alone, I wouldn't have said anything. But now I had the sergeant as a witness and there was no going back. We tied him up right there. The next morning I left everything in my superiors' hands. Nevertheless, I did tell them we hadn't found anything on him and he might be more useful to us alive.

My attempts were in vain and they executed him the next morning. The captain told me to give the order to the firing squad. He fell shouting *Viva la República!* And they made me put the final shot in his head.

I looked at the woman out of the corner of my eye, but she kept telling me about her husband's ups and downs as if she hadn't noticed anything. Did she know anything? Was she toying with me? My full attention was on the fact that, after twenty-three years, the soldier in the photo and I had become very different. I have a beard now, and once the war was over my hair quickly went white. I consoled myself thinking the woman couldn't have recognized me, but I was still uneasy.

I immediately tried to talk about something else and lead the conversation in another direction, and the woman also realized she had spent more time than usual with me and the cats would be waiting for her by now.

When she left, I was still thinking and now I understood why I had thought I recognized the name of the boarding house in the guidebook my boss had given me. Hôtel Virenque, Rue Mouffetard. Marcel had mentioned it many times.

That night, I opened the wardrobe, got out the newspapers the woman had gathered up with such care that first day and spread them out on the table. I started to read them one by one. They were from just after the liberation of Paris. They had all kinds of news. Including a fire at the Virenque hotel on Mouffetard street.

I took the papers and went to the taxidermist's room. I knocked at the door and the woman immediately flew out from within, saying *"chui désolée, chui désolée"* and doing up the buttons at her breast. The bed was unmade and I caught a glimpse of the one-armed man in his long underwear, bewilderment etched on his brow. We stopped and stared at each other for a moment. On top of a table, I saw Kitty with a long gash in his belly, lying among many tools with a pile of straw nearby. Now I was the one repeating *"chui désolé,"* and I left.

I couldn't bear to learn any more.

The next morning I had breakfast out so I wouldn't run into them. In the afternoon, the woman came to me with a letter. She didn't mention what had happened the day before. She told me she would let me read the last letter her husband had written to her before he died. I was afraid my name would be in it somewhere, so I scanned it quickly from top to bottom first without reading it through, looking for my name. I calmed down then and, before reading the letter I held in my hands, held out the newspapers to her with no fear now. I would understand if she didn't want to tell me about it, but I had seen that piece of news and wondered what it was. She told me. It had all happened because she had had some tall blond men staying at her boarding house. Very nice men, even if she didn't really understand everything they said. She ironed their uniforms and gladly washed their clothes and things. But one day they had to leave. Then people came to her boarding house and hauled her out onto the streets. They shaved her head for being a collaborator and mocked her, marching her through the neighborhood streets. And they set fire to her house. "Thank God for Gérard! Thanks to him I was able to rebuild all this." But she told me to forget these stories and read the letter. It said ordinary things. The usual things any husband would say to his wife in such a situation. At the end, he thanked her for the last pair of socks and asked her for a sweater, *if at all possible,* since the winter would be hard.

LOURDES OÑEDERRA (Donostia, 1958)

My first formal, special and purposeful relationship with literature came about before I'd finished my studies in Spanish philology, when I wrote what would become the epilogue to Ramon Saizarbitoria's *Ehun Metro* (*A Hundred Meters*). Around the same I time met Saizarbitoria himself: him and the people who were part of his literary circle, the writers of the magazine *Oh Euzkadi*; and I am especially indebted to that time, that atmosphere, and to Ramon in particular for making me believe that I had to write. Also, before I completed my degree I started writing reviews for the magazine *Ere*, with Andu Lertxundi as my boss.

I don't know for sure when it happened, but I know that by the time I got my degree, in 1980, and went to the United States to do a masters in linguistics, it was entirely clear to me that I would not study any more literature; I had developed a terror of it by then. Studying literature, I felt, would extinguish whatever it was that since childhood had made me ceaselessly put things into words and words on paper. Since that time, I've dedicated my professional life to studying, researching and teaching phonology. In between, I've written for *Egunkaria* and *Hika* about contemporary issues such as our language and our political situation.

But through the cracks something else escapes, and when I sit down to work seriously with it, the stories come out. That is how, struggling over several long years, I wrote the novel *...Eta emakumeari sugeak esan zion* (1999, *...And the Snake Told the Woman*). And since its success I've published the story *Anderson andrearen kutixia* (2000, *Mrs. Anderson's longing*), and have also been commissioned to write for several magazines.

Nowadays, my work in phonology is inescapably leading me to study the rhythms of the language, and that has had an intimate impact on the writing I was hoping to keep separate from my professional work.

Mrs Anderson's Longing

by

LOURDES OÑEDERRA

Translated by Amaia Gabantxo

To Evelyn and Dennis, with thanks.

An evening in April, and it was still light.
(Doris Lessing, *Love, Again*).

Nothing is more attractive than sensing the effect of one's attractiveness on others. That was surely the reason (thought Mrs. Anderson), why she had been so successful with men in her youth. In her youth. A long time ago. A long time ago, in her youth, men used to like Mrs. Anderson a lot, young men especially, because she also used to like men a lot (and nothing is more attractive than sensing the effect of one's attractiveness on others). She wasn't ugly in her youth. That must also have helped, although there were prettier girls around, in her parish. In any case, she was the most successful one. Back then she had even found the game too easy sometimes.

That's why she had to marry Mr. Anderson, because Mr. Anderson hadn't fallen in love with her as easily as the others.

She mistook Mr. Anderson's apathy for true love and, since she married Mr. Anderson, Mrs. Anderson hadn't loved another man, hadn't felt attracted to any other man. She didn't think about it, it didn't worry her at all. Mr. Anderson's good points made up for his apathy and Mrs. Anderson was happy for many years. Happy while bringing up the children she and Mr. Anderson had together, happy while Mr. Anderson made money, happy while she kept their grand house for him, while she tended the garden.

She didn't love any other man, she didn't need another man. Mrs. Anderson still thinks she leads a happy life.

As the children grew, during all those years when Mr. Anderson made money (lots of money), Mr. and Mrs. Anderson came to an agreement to follow certain rules neither of them ever voiced. Mrs. Anderson would take care of all household matters: she would decide what her husband and children should wear at any given occasion, the color of the living room wall, what they ate, whom to invite to their Thanksgiving party and how many towels to bring to the beach. At all other times she always did what her husband said, always accepted his orders. Seldom, very seldom did they argue. Or so it seems now to Mrs. Anderson.

But there was one thing that when seen from the outside seemed rather peculiar (although the Andersons never noticed it, of course). This was Mr. Anderson's rule about flying. At some point (Mrs. Anderson can't remember exactly when), Mr. Anderson decided that he and his wife would never board the same flight. In this way, if ever anything happened, their children would not be orphaned (*completely* orphaned, that is).

On that account too Mrs. Anderson had no doubts at all, she never started an argument, she never felt the need. When her husband mentioned his decision to her for the first time... so long ago now... yes, now Mrs.

Anderson recalls. The children were old enough to be without her for a few days, the nanny could look after them (the youngest must have been three years old) and, when they decided that she too would go to her husband's meeting in Chicago, Mr. Anderson's precaution seemed completely reasonable to Mrs. Anderson. Bit by bit, year by year, flight after flight, that too (like so many other things) became a habit, and now it seems the most natural thing in the world. One more silent rule in the small world of the Anderson marriage. She almost finds it strange when at airports or in planes, she notices couples that look like they might be parents.

But that's enough daydreaming; now Mrs. Anderson has to open the telephone book to look for Tim's number. She puts her glasses on, pushing them up the bridge of her nose, closer to her eyes. Tim, Tim, Tim. There he is: Tim. Just like that, no surname. Nothing else: Tim. As soon as she reads the line of numbers she thinks it seems familiar to her and this is not so surprising after all, because although she only calls him once a year, she does ring him every year. Every year for a long time. It must be ten years now that she's been ringing Tim every spring. Ever since Mr. Anderson's heart attack; or rather since his second heart attack. Her husband was 62 then. She was 60. That frightening operation. That was twelve years ago. Mrs. Anderson counts the years one by one, every single spring, one by one. It must be ten or eleven years since she started calling Tim in the spring.

Mr. Anderson goes to Germany every spring, where they clean his blood in an expensive German hospital. Following his diktat, in total accordance with his decision, Mr. Anderson travels on one plane and Mrs. Anderson on another. Not only that, but Mrs. Anderson leaves a few days after him and arrives in Germany a few days later. During that period they do the usual tests on Mr. Anderson and (since he doesn't stay in the hospital overnight in the meantime) he makes sure the hotel room meets his wife's needs. He has always looked after his wife, protected her from the strange wide world. His sweet wife among all these rough Germans. They know the Andersons at the hotel and most years they give them the same room, but sometimes the room is taken, and once they were given one that was too noisy. His wife is used to the Californian mildness, to her quiet garden. What do Germans know, or Europeans for that matter.

Mrs. Anderson can't remember how she managed to fly later that first time. Perhaps there weren't any tickets, or maybe she said that as an excuse. No, she was sure she hadn't lied to Mr. Anderson. Something to do with the children. Maybe it was because their daughter was about to get married and she needed to help her choose her gown. Who knows. What's certain is that she flew a few days later than her husband.

Since then the ritual has always been the same:

A. Mr. Anderson rings the German hospital to make an appointment, to double check his appointment. Every year the charming voice that answers the phone is surprised because he doesn't immediately give his name. Dry Europeans.

B. Mr. and Mrs. Anderson buy their tickets to Europe. Always at the same travel agents. Each for a different flight, each for a different date.

C. Mrs. Anderson rings Tim and says that her husband is leaving on such and such a day. That she is leaving on such and such a day. Will he come to prune the trees in the garden. To get them ready for the summer.

D. Mr. Anderson leaves, with the suitcase his wife has packed for him. Often he takes a taxi to the airport, at least the last few times. Before that Mrs. Anderson used to take him sometimes. On a couple of occasions his son has taken him too (he comes down south sometimes for work reasons; their daughter lives in Washington with her kids).

E. Mrs. Anderson opens the front door to Tim, shortly after the plane leaves the airport.

Once a year. Every year.

Tim is older than he was when he started to come. Ten or eleven years older. He is older, but still hasn't started to age. He must be around fifty. The wrinkles in his face have made him handsomer. His mouth stands out more, the softness of his fleshy lips is more pronounced. Ten years ago he only had a few gray hairs. Now his hair has turned almost completely white. Because of the whiteness of his hair, however, the healthy sheen of his face looks darker, is more noticeable. But it's Tim's muscles that Mrs. Anderson likes best. Or the eyes, maybe the eyes. The all-encompassing blueness of Tim's small eyes, the fugitive moistness in the folds of his wrinkles.

Not all men grow more beautiful with age. Most men just wither away, soften, look battered. That, or they become fat (or fat and red). Tim is almost always outdoors, out in the sun, in the open air. That is why he's got those healthy, mature good looks women are always so glad to encounter in a man. Those good looks.

This year too she must ring Tim. Her yearly nervous moment. Her yearly pleasure, her little secret, her sin, her longing: Tim's voice on the phone, and then, a few days later, opening the door to Tim.

Tim's smile, before he starts work, when she offers him some coffee.

Tim's muscular arms, when he takes the ladder out of the garage.

Tim's round buttocks inside the faded jeans, up the ladder.

Tim's eyes looking at the branches that need pruning.

Mrs. Anderson watches Tim work from the window. Mostly from the kitchen window, because most of the trees Tim prunes are on that side. Sometimes she's outside as well, with the pretext of tending to the flowers, or sitting on the porch, when the weather is good (pretending to read the letters she's just collected from the mailbox).

Most times the weather is good when Tim comes, because he comes during the spring and the weather is good in California during the spring. The weather is almost always good in California.

Tim is not from California, but he's lived in California for a long time. Like many others he came during the hippy days and he's never left. The California climate, the beauty and relaxed lifestyle of California grabbed hold of him.

A sudden downpour is possible too during a California spring. Mrs. Anderson likes it when Tim is pruning the branches and it starts to rain all of a sudden. That way, Tim has to stop working for a while and come into the kitchen. Mrs. Anderson loves to talk with Tim, to have Tim closer, to play with Tim's eyes, to say something stupid and watch how Tim's lips break up into the sweetest of smiles. Tim's eyes almost disappear. A moist blue line among tanned folds.

Some years (most) it doesn't rain and Tim doesn't come into the kitchen to talk and smile to her. Those years she looks at Tim from a distance (for longer), and Tim doesn't look at her as much. It doesn't matter. The safety of the distance gives Mrs. Anderson the chance to look at Tim as much as she likes.

On such occasions Tim smiles at Mrs. Anderson too. Sometimes he even laughs out loud because of a sudden memory, or because he drops a tool, or because he sees a neighbor jogging down the lane in designer flower-patterned pants. Tim is a very cheerful man. At least that is what Mrs. Anderson thinks.

But Tim isn't always cheerful.

When he remembers his California of thirty years ago, at least most of the times he does, he doesn't feel very cheerful. He gets sad on such occasions, on most of them at least. Remembering many of his pot-smoking friends of that period fills him with an unease that's close to anger. Not because they're lost. Not because he doesn't know where they are, or whether they exist anymore. But because of the yuppies in the banks and multinationals. And it's not because he now finds them wealthy and boring. He doesn't care if they are boring, he doesn't have to put up with them. The money issue doesn't bother him too much either. He wouldn't have chosen the path he's chosen if he'd wanted money. He lives happily with what his sporadic jobs pay him. He makes more than enough to live in his trailer on the hilly coast (on the bit above the beach) and to buy gas for his old red car; and he has all the time in the world to do what he likes best: to play the harmonica while looking out over the sea. What makes him sick to his stomach about these ex-hippies-now-yuppies is the looks of pity they give him. That he can't stand.

But anyhow, he doesn't often dwell on this sort of thing. He forgets about them. He has to forget them. He pays for this peace with his loneliness. Loneliness is the price. He has almost no friends. Every now and then a girlfriend. Younger and younger ones. No, it's him who's getting older and older. On Saturday nights at the bar, surrounded by mellow country music, with a beer in his hand, he never finds women of his own age, or not the kind he'd like to spend the night with, anyway (an accomplice with whom to fritter away the loneliness of the night, at least once a week).

Mrs. Anderson is one of his few friends. His once-a-year friend, his once-a-year customer, his once-a-year mother – his own lost her welcoming smile a long time ago. Vietnam. Those who didn't want to go to war burnt their passports, like feminists burnt their bras. He hasn't been to his parents' home since, only for his grandparents' funerals. Mrs. Anderson's smile every spring is his yearly blessing.

Mrs. Anderson's yearly blessing, smile, and check, are the handsomest payments of his entire year (no one is as generous as Mrs. Anderson). He'll invite red-haired Cathy to the restaurant by the beach. They'll drink white wine. They'll eat oysters. Cathy loves tempura oysters. He thinks that's the perfect way to ruin oysters, but he doesn't say anything. He likes seeing Cathy happy, to watch her eat oysters at least once a year. Cathy is worse off than him. She has smoked everything, she has put all sorts of things into her skinny body. Tim thinks about red-haired Cathy's prematurely aged skin while he stretches his right hand towards a branch, to hold it.

Mrs. Anderson has gone up to the bedroom. She has to start packing her suitcase. She'll be going to Germany the day after tomorrow. She must pack her suitcase. In case she needs to buy something, too, she'd better have a look now and she what she needs to bring. She doesn't like having to buy things in Europe. She can't figure out how. Nothing is the same, nothing is as trustworthy as the stuff at home.

In five weeks the Andersons will be back here again. Mr. Anderson will return the day after her. By then she will have bought fruit and vegetables and the house will be ready, everything will be in order, everything will be cozy and perfect (unless the Mexican maid leaves something undone or unmade...)

Mr. Anderson will find the trees have been pruned.

The pruned branches will be gathered and piled up by the garage. Before, he used to do that job every year. Even if one of those companies that look after gardens used to send a gardener every week, the spring pruning used to be his job. He would do the job one weekend in the spring. He would gather up the pruned branches and (after chopping them into regular-sized logs) pile up by the garage the amount they would need to burn during the winter months.

After the first heart attack, Mrs. Anderson told him once that it might not be good for him to do that job. She only told him once. That the doctor had said to be careful and not to exert himself physically. Mr. Anderson replied that the job did him good, it relaxed him and he didn't have to exert himself that much in order to cut the branches and pile them up (evenly chopped) by the garage. Mrs. Anderson never said anything again and he continued to do that job every spring (until he had his second heart attack).

Since Mr. Anderson had his second heart attack he hasn't needed to prune any branches. By the time he returns from the hospital in Germany the branches are pruned, chopped, gathered and piled up. In the winter, when they light the fire in the living room to warm and decorate the room (even in the winter it isn't really cold in California), he carries a dozen logs from the garage to the fireplace in a small basket. Mr. Anderson has never asked who prunes the trees.

Since Mr. Anderson had the second heart attack, Mrs. Anderson does little apart from looking after her husband.

Mr. Anderson has quietened down since his second heart attack. He lets his wife love him. Look after him.

Since Mr. Anderson had his second heart attack, Tim comes to prune the trees every year.

Yearly pleasure. Yearly secret. Mrs. Anderson's longing.

IXIAR ROZAS (Lasarte-Oria, 1972)

Even though the love of reading led me to write, when I first began being a reader I never in any way imagined that I would become—that huge word—a writer. It was on the assumption that it would have something to do with letters and with life that I chose to study journalism in Iruñea (Pamplona). On the way, though, real letters and real life made me look to Barcelona. In that city, thanks to a fellowship, I wrote *Edo zu edo ni* (2000, *Either You or I*), my first novel. The poetry collection *Patio bat bi itsasoen artean* (2001, *A Courtyard Between the Two Seas*, Ernestina Champourcin Prize) was also written in Barcelona.

When I returned to the Basque Country, I wrote the young-adult books *Yako* (2001) and *Izurderen bidaia* (2001, *Dolphin's Voyage*), while writing for grownups the linked stories in the volume *Sartu, korrontea dabil* (2001, *Come In, There's a Draft*). The book begins with "A Draft, a Current," ne story that follows. Several of my stories have been anthologized. In the meantime, I've written scripts for television and radio, and two plays, both unpublished. The last work I've published is the young-adult book *Yako eta haizea* (2002, *Yako and the Wind*). *Sartu, korrontea dabil* recently appeared in Spanish translation, as *Luego les separa la noche* (2003, *So the Night Divides Them*).

May the reader who takes pleasure in writing take pleasure in what I've written. Place life, existence, in doubt; always holding to the need to look inward, in this society that obliges us to live looking outward.

A Draft

by

IXIAR ROZAS

Translated by Elizabeth Macklin and Linda White

"Excuse me, would you close the door please?"

The woman isn't asking Abdou, but rather the man sitting next to the door. Sometimes the woman dozes off, but she awakes with a start when her head nods. When she opens her eyes, Abdou sees that they're watery, and he turns his gaze back to the window. Once when her head nods, it lands on Abdou's shoulder. Her dark hair is very smooth, it looks like a child's, but the lines on her face make her look forty. She smells good, she has a unique scent. She doesn't wear cheap perfume like the village girls when they're out for boys. Abdou gently removes her head from his shoulder and leans it against the window.

The man sitting by the door has his eyes on a book. Every time the train is in a station, he lifts them to the window and sighs, as if he wants everything he's reading about to be reflected in the window. He also glances at the door from time to time, to make sure it's closed. He's dressed in black from head to foot. Black like the rain falling outside the window.

Ever since he was old enough to understand, Abdou had heard that rain has the power to grant wishes.

Before he got on the train, no one told him there would be so much rain. They said where to go to catch the train and how long the trip would be, but not a word about the rain. Evidently, it hadn't seemed worth mentioning to those who gave him the information he needed to make the trip. No knowledge of rain was exchanged for the money he'd paid.

This detail is important to him though, because the success or failure of what he's about to do may lie in the rain. At least, if what he's heard about the power of the rain is true.

Abdou has just turned nineteen. He's headed for an unfamiliar city, to Paris, a name he has heard all his life on the tongues of his countrymen. He's traveling by train now, because they told him it was the surest way of avoiding unpleasant surprises. But before that, he traveled in every way possible, on foot, by ship — if an undersized launch could be called a ship — and in the back of a refrigerator truck. He traveled night and day in the company of other young men, all of them going in search of a better life. Fortunately, when he looked into their faces Abdou saw that he himself was different, because he was not searching for a better life. He was going to Paris for no other reason than to bring honor to his name.

It's been days since he bade farewell to his country, Mali. As he said goodbye, he looked into his mother's eyes and prayed that he might find his father. In his pocket, along with his father's photograph, he carried the address of a restaurant written on a piece of paper, the starting point of his search. It was said all Malians gathered there once a week, and they could certainly set him

on his father's trail. That was his only hope because without their help, he didn't know where else to turn.

Word had come to him that they last saw Abdou's
father in a Parisian train station. The restaurant owner
reported that he was carrying a large suitcase, which
could have meant he was leaving or arriving, but then the
owner saw him catch a taxi, so he was coming to stay.
Another compatriot in search of a better life, that's what
the restaurant owner was thinking. By the time he got
close to the taxi, it was pulling away. No chance to greet
the new arrival. Nor had they seen him since. It was possible he had left the city, or perhaps had simply disappeared into its maze of streets and houses as do so many
city dwellers. That was all they could say.

Abdou is certain that will not happen to him. He'll
return home to his country. He's been thinking about
that since he sat down on the train, everything made easier by its movement along the rails. Or maybe he was
thinking it because of a dozen other reasons, because he
was mixed in with other people all traveling together. For
now, Abdou is just another person in the compartment,
different from the man and woman on either side of him
but gazing out the window like someone who makes the
journey every day, forgetting all about the photograph in
his pocket. He paid for a ticket just like the others. He's
not bad looking. He's wearing the beautiful shirt his
mother bought him. Only the darkness of his skin makes
him stand out, but that's nothing to worry about, for in
Paris there are many dark-skinned people like him.

Suddenly, the woman gets up, puts on her coat and
goes into the corridor, holding a cell pone. The reader's
eyes are glued to his book, glancing down now and then
at the black suitcase between his feet. The dark-haired

woman is beautiful, she's wearing red lipstick and is elegantly dressed. She folds her arms across her middle, as if her coat were not enough to warm her body. She takes a few drags on the cigarette and returns to the compartment, just as another young man enters. If he were dark-skinned, he'd look a lot like Abdou. But there's a big difference between the two of the them. Unlike Abdou, the newcomer chose his destination randomly.

"Is this seat free?" asks the young man, glancing around the compartment.

He asks with a smile. The three of them nod yes, the woman mechanically, Abdou pleasantly, and the reader without lifting his eyes from his book. He only glances sideways as the rough-looking newcomer enters. The newcomer carries a case. So does the woman, but his isn't a briefcase, it's a case for a musical instrument, a guitar, a violin, or a viola, one of those.

For a second, it feels like Abdou and the young man are all alone in the compartment, the way they look at each other, long and hard, taking each other's measure. Then Abdou turns his gaze back to the window. Although in his country it was relatively common for men to sleep with men, Abdou loves women. He would be happy to spend night after night embracing the sweet-smelling brunette at his side, nibbling at her delicate lips.

The compartment door is left open again.

"Excuse me, would you close the door please? There's a draft, and I wouldn't want to get a chill," says the woman as pleasantly as possible.

She folds her arms across her middle again. Her eyes are closing, as if she guessed Abdou's thoughts and wants to flee from them. The landscape outside the window is green. That generous landscape whizzing by is so different from the stingy flatlands of his own country. The landscape there looks like the wrinkled skin of an old man. Here it seems fluffy, like a baby's curly hair.

There are so many things Abdou does not understand. Why are there so many obstacles to getting anywhere? Why does he have to move like a snake in the dirt, risking his life, if the big nations have already stolen everything they need from his country?

And the one question that stands out above all others: Why have you done all of this to us?

That's a question Abdou would like to ask the others in the train compartment. Would they have any answers? But then, who is he to barge into the lives of such peaceful people? He prefers to believe that one of these days everything will be easier, although ever since he was old enough to understand, he heard that power grows on the backs of the small, and his country could still become much more diminished. Nevertheless, he truly believes that something is changing in his own life, and it's better to believe in small things than big ones. In order to change the big things, you have to begin with the small ones, and that's just what he'll do when he finds his father's trail.

Perhaps the rain will help him.

It was raining that morning he woke up and found his mother crying. It was no wonder he remembered that rain, for in his country it only rains once or twice a year. Add the fact that his father left home that morning, and Abdou was bound to remember the rain. A father leaves for good once in a lifetime, or maybe twice, but if he comes back and leaves a second time there is no third chance. That's what Abdou had heard since he was old enough to understand.

That's why, in the beginning, Abdou thought his father would return and his mother's tears were caused by something else. He thought she was crying for joy because his father had gone away to bring back a baby. His mother's hidden desire was to have another baby. Abdou's hidden desire was revealed when he spoke to her sweetly, saying, "Don't worry, he'll be home by nightfall."

Abdou spoke tenderly to his mother in his capacity as eldest brother. It was his duty. However, he was unable to soothe her distress. Tears darkened her face with the same power of the water that furrowed the dry earth. Her hands trembled and so did the paper she held. The silence was so pervasive he could even hear the paper trembling. At last, staring into space, his mother ended the silence.

"He's gone. He's gone and left us, Abdou."

She appended her son's name at the end, for he was the only hope left to her. Abdou returned to his bedroom, scowling at the rain through the open window. Smoke seemed to rise from the earth, a tussle between the heat and the rain. Smoke poured out of the bedroom, too. Abdou had rolled a cigarette and was smoking furiously.

He was only fifteen then. Four years passed before the morning when he learned his mother was sick.

"Go look for him, Abdou," she insisted. "I don't want to leave you all by yourselves when I die."

She was speaking of her seven sons and daughters. As the eldest, Abdou knew that his mother had never spoken with such grim determination before. Something was about to happen. He could lose no time. He would do everything in his power to find his father.

The woman gets up from her seat, and the noise brings Abdou back to the train. She picks up her small black case and goes into the corridor. She takes her phone, presses the buttons, and waits. Then nervously, she begins to speak as if her life were draining from her with every utterance. Somberly, she ends the call. Then she makes another, more serenely. A smile appears on her face while she waits for someone to answer. From her case, she takes out a diary and opens it.

Abdou is not the only one watching the woman. The reader watches her, too. But the newcomer is a prisoner of his own thoughts, or perhaps of the instrument in his case. The woman ends the second call. She picks up her case, lights another cigarette, and moves along the corridor. She takes a long drag and stands looking out the window. Lights from the highway outside are reflected in her face, light and shadow, light and shadow. She's one of those women who thinks twice before making decisions. Another drag on the cigarette, another thought.

"Excuse me, would you close the door please? There's a draft."

The words hang in the air. She has a weighty voice that gives each word immense importance, unlike the lighter, quicker voice of the newcomer. Just as he randomly chose Paris over any other destination, his voice made one word seem like any other. He hasn't spoken again since he entered the compartment.

"Are you married? Do you have any children?"

Abdou would like to ask those questions. He'd like to know if having a husband was the reason for her teary eyes, if she had just called him. The reader now gazes at Abdou's old traveling bag as if trying to guess what is inside. But he never could because it is full of the mementos and photos that Abdou had brought along to convince his father to return home.

"If you rekindle his memories, he'll come back," his mother announced as she packed her chosen mementos into his bag.

"And if I don't find him, mother, what then?" Abdou asks himself now.

When the woman reenters the compartment, the reader returns to his book as if embarrassed to have been looking at Abdou. It crosses Abdou's mind that the woman might be having her period. Abdou's sense of smell is highly developed and he knows that menstruating women have a different scent. But the sweet smell of her perfume wins out and he can detect no other. He'd have to be closer to her to be sure. If she puts her head on his shoulder again, he will inhale more deeply. For now, he concentrates totally on what he's about to say.

"Will it be long before we arrive?" Abdou dares to ask.

He believes that questions are often a way of getting closer to strangers. The newcomer shakes his head no with a smile. The other two, however, seem far, far away from the train compartment. Abdou feels that quite a few hours have passed since the departure, so it's possible that it won't be long now, as the newcomer suggests. He takes the photo of his father out of his pocket and dares to ask another question, almost afraid to breathe.

"Do any of you know him?" Timidly. "He's my father."

The three of them turn to look at the photo. Silently, they examine it. Abdou needs only the faintest positive sign to feel his journey is not useless, but the silence continues. At last, with a hopeless gesture, the newcomer says he's sorry, but he hasn't been in the city for years.

The woman remarks, "Finding someone in Paris is as impossible as believing in fate."

Again, her words hang heavy in the air. She glances sideways at the photo, at the undeniable resemblance between father and son.

The woman would take pleasure in telling Abdou that the man might not be his father. He can only be sure of his mother. He'll never know if his father is for real. That's the way life is in big cities like Paris. She would also tell him to go home to his country if he wants to avoid the city's clutches. And while she's thinking that, their eyes meet and linger for the first time. Sparks fly. She thinks she could lose herself in his lips for a long night.

"No, I've never seen him. I'm very sorry, very sorry," as if the repetition it will convince herself, and she shakes her head no.

Her eyes are an unknown color, since for dark-skinned people no color is more unfamiliar than blue, like the Mali sky on a dark night. Abdou has known that, too, for a long time.

Silence descends on the compartment, a silence broken only by the sound of the rails, shutting out even the smallest word of cheer.

The newcomer begins to whistle. He could take his instrument from its case and start playing right now. The reader has his eyes on his book, and the woman looks out the window. She combs her fingers through her long hair, opening wide spaces between the strands. Through them, Abdou sees that the light from the window is brighter now. They are undoubtedly entering a city much larger than any they have passed through thus far. As soon as he's off the train, he'll have a taxi driver take him to the address on the paper he carries.

The train is slowing down. The woman uses a hand mirror to touch up her makeup. Then she stands up, leaves the compartment, and starts talking on the phone. Just as before, she makes the first call with a taut face, and the second with a smile.

She still hasn't returned to her seat. She's standing in the corridor, thoughtful, watching the night lights of the city. Abdou scoots closer to the window. He sees the iron roof of the station and, reflected in the glass, his own exhausted face, limned with the fear that a few days in this city will turn into months, and the months into years. That's what has happened to everyone who left Mali.

The newcomer caresses the side of his instrument case, eager to put his fingers to the strings. The reader closes his book and sighs, for he won't be able to read again until he's finally home. Or perhaps he is bored with the book, maybe it has failed to capture his attention. The woman in the corridor lights a cigarette.

The train slows even more. Abdou sees the large station clock. It's ten p.m. But he wasn't expecting what he saw beneath the clock. They told him the train was the safest way to travel, that nothing would happen to him, but they also told him to go by night. He hoped the shirt his mother bought him would make him less conspicuous. Beads of perspiration run down his temples. Plainclothes policemen are on the platform waiting for the moment they'll make an arrest.

The woman reenters the compartment. She looks straight at Abdou as if to ask how he will avoid the police. The reader stows his book in his bag and the new-comer doesn't even notice the police presence. His gaze and consciousness are elsewhere.

The woman offers Abdou a cigarette. Their hands touch as she brings the lighter flame toward him. Abdou, however, is unable to smile a thank you. The woman lifts her suitcase from the metal shelf above her head. The reader also picks up his bag, a wheeled suitcase. The new-comer cradles his instrument case under his arm.

But Abdou remains in his seat. If it were raining the rain that grants wishes, he would beg the train not to stop, to retrace all the miles that have brought him here. But the station is huge and the sheltering roof prevents him from seeing whether it's raining.

The three others move toward the door of the car and wait to see who will be first to step through. The sudden light of the station reveals Abdou's fear.

The train has come to a complete stop. Abdou has no choice but to stand and sling his bag over his shoulder. The woman pauses and lets the reader go ahead of her.

On the platform, one of the policemen peers intently at everyone who gets off the train. The reader goes down the steps, and the newcomer follows him, casting a glance at Abdou as if wanting him to know that at last he understands everything. Abdou wants to retrace his steps, but it's too late. It's the woman's turn to descend the steps and Abdou follows her as his eyes catch the policeman's shrewd smile. Then, in a split second, the woman takes Abdou's arm.

"My husband is quite slow," she says to the police-man, without hesitation. "Come, darling, our little girl is waiting."

She plants a light kiss on Abdou's cheek but says no more. They descend from the car arm in arm. Abdou is speechless. He can't believe what is happening. The woman holds tightly to his arm. He is under her control, entirely at her service.

The suspicious policeman watches the couple for a second, a word on the tip of his tongue. But instead he says something to his partner, and they go on with their surveillance.

The reader sees it all. He almost said something, but instead prefers to watch the momentary couple disappear through the station entrance. He has never read anything like this in his books. The newcomer sits down on a random bench, waiting.

As they leave the station, Abdou notices that it's raining. The woman makes sure the police are no longer watching, then releases his arm. He smiles at her, a smile full of gratitude and instant loyalty. They share a goodbye glance.

The woman gives the man who waits for her a light kiss on the lips. They get on a motorcycle and disappear in the distance.

Abdou hails a cab and takes the address from his pocket. The driver is unwelcoming at first, but as soon as he sees that Abdou has the money to pay for the ride, he tells him to get in. Abdou looks at his bag. He looks at the leather seat of the taxi. The rain washes the sweat from his temples and he climbs into the taxi. He takes his seat and shows the driver the photo of his father. The city rushes past the window.

JOSEBA SARRIONANDIA (Iurreta, 1958)

Graduate in Basque Philology, contributor to many journals, translator, associate member of the Basque Academy, co-founder of the literary group POTT Banda, Joseba Sarrionandia was imprisoned for being a member of ETA from 1980 until his escape in 1985. There are few writers who, in addition to the usual genres (poetry, narrative, essay), have published as many innovative hybrid texts as Sarrionandia. Among his books of fiction, philosophy and literary criticism, *Ni ez naiz hemengoa* (1985, *I am Not of Here*), *Marginalia* (1988) *Ez gara geure baitakoak* (1989, *We are Not of Ourselves*), *Han izanik huna naiz* (1992, *Having Been There, Here I Am*) and *Hitzen ondoeza* (1997, *The Malaise of Words*) stand out; his translations include T. S. Eliot's *The Waste Land*, F. Pessoa's *O Marinheiro* and S. T. Coleridge's *The Rime of the Ancient Mariner*. Sarrionandia has shown himself to be a tireless traveler in literary geographies, an ancient mariner dazzled by an ocean of ideas. *Narrazioak* (1983, *Narrations*), *Atabala eta euria* (1986, *The Drum and the Rain*) and *Ifar Aldeko orduak* (1991, *Northern Times*) are his best known books of short stories. English-speaking readers can read and listen to his charming anthology of poems and letters in the book *Hau da ene ondasun guzia* (1999, *This is all I Have*). (M. J. Olaziregi)

Alone

by

JOSEBA SARRIONANDIA

Translated by Linda White

She's alone in the world.

She loves getting letters, but when she looks in the mailbox it's always empty.

She decided to write to herself. She put the letter in an envelope and wrote her address on it twice, once as the recipient and once as the sender.

She went out for a walk down the empty streets and dropped the letter in a random city mailbox. She has been waiting ever since, for two or three days. Every morning she looks in her mailbox. The letter hasn't arrived.

She is truly alone in the world.

The Treasure Chest

by

JOSEBA SARRIONANDIA

Translated by Linda White

Once upon a time, far far away, there was an explorer who was hunting for treasure. He spent twenty years digging furiously with pick and shovel, looking for a treasure chest full of gold. Then he spent another twenty years doing the same thing with incredible perseverance, sweating buckets, but all in vain.

Instead of giving up, he went on for another twenty years digging holes, and at last, sparks flew when his pick struck the copper fittings of a treasure chest. He pulled the big, beautiful, tightly locked object out of the ground. It was no small task to break the lock.

But when he managed to open the chest, there was nothing inside but ashes. And once he had emptied it, what did he do but die!

Since he'd never earned enough money in his life to buy a coffin or a mausoleum, they put him in that cramped chest all curled up, with his toes nearly in his mouth, and they buried him. It didn't make a bad wooden overcoat...

And there he remained, with no stone or marker, like all treasures that are hard to find.

The Ancient Mariner

by

JOSEBA SARRIONANDIA

Translated by Linda White

"Sooner or later everyone knows
All the routes of escape are closed."

Joannes Etxeberri of Ziburu

A cluster of old houses surrounded an ivy-covered church at the foot of a terrible cliff on the steep seaward slope. Narrow paths led down to the port. No railway served these smugglers' stores, and there was no road for cars. The smuggler had to travel on foot or by mule, and on my bosses' orders, I set out on foot as well.

Seagulls coming to shore is the sign of a storm, and they'd been flying over my head since I reached the coast. By the time I set eyes on the Cantabrian Sea, there was thunder overhead, looming dark over the mountains and the waves. At dusk I began to run along the empty pathways, slipping on the dirty stones. My bosses told me there would be a small, solitary inn facing the port, and inside I would find an old fisherman. My errand was with him.

I came into the town, down to the dock, and into the dark old inn with its glazed windows. I saw the man I wanted at a worn wooden table, sitting alone. Wrinkles and a white beard. No strangers must ever come in there because he recognized me at once and invited me to sit.

"They say a storm is coming," he said, peering into my eyes. "Did you see it from the hill?"

"Yes. I had to run all the way down," I replied.

"A black storm."

The bartender lit an oil lamp. Now the old man's dark eyes looked blue to me. There was surely a big storm coming. Mariners' wives were standing at their windows with worried faces. We could see them through the windows of the inn. Also visible was the murky, churning sea, and there was not a single fisherman on its dark and choppy surface.

The bartender brought gin for the old salt and red wine for me, both in heavy glasses. The mariner lifted his glass roughly.

"The sea's a cup, an avenger stirred up," he said.

Gin splashed on the table. I wondered if he was drunk, but something else glinted in his blue eyes.

I asked the bartender if he had a room available for the night, and he said yes. Today, at least, I knew I would have dry sheets.

As I wiped off the window with my neckerchief, the woman who'd appeared at hers left the house and went to the dock with a child in her arms.

There, more women had gathered. They conversed nervously. From the bar you could only hear a few isolated words.

"Afraid of turning into widows," said the old man, watching them.

The women, some holding babies, gazed out at the dark sea but saw nothing.

Our conversation drifted to life on the water, and we reminisced with deep sadness. We had both spent long periods at sea and got to know many ports. I didn't want to tell him the reason I'd come. The smuggling. I knew the old man hadn't been to sea for a long, long time.

In the city, a terrible story was being passed around. I didn't know if it was true or not, and I didn't mention it, but with each glass we drew nearer to the subject. The rain was falling gently against the window, the sound of it a background to the sailor's voice.

"There were three of us working, my brother, my son, and me. A white whale came close to shore and we got it in our heads to go after him. Not just to get the whale. We were betting on who was the best harpooner. We went out in the long-boat and overtook it easily because it was sick. It came to shore to die. We harpooned it, but it was a big whale, and he fought hard to get away. He thrashed about in the water, and it took us two hours to finish him off."

"We got a whale once, too, in the Irish Sea," I said, "but didn't have the room or the time to haul it in, so it stayed right where it was, like a small island on the water."

The old man continued, "We kept arguing over who had done more to kill the whale, since it took all three of us to do it. Meanwhile, like you said, it was floating there like a smooth-surfaced island. And three seagulls circled over it, birds as eternal as the heavens, and they lit on top of the dead whale. One of us said, 'Look at the gulls. Now we'll see who's best with the harpoon.' Then each of us hurled a harpoon at a gull, and we were damn good. We hit them, and they plunged into the water in mid-screech. But mine was stuck on the harpoon. I pulled in the line, and my hands were soaked in its warm blood when I took it off the barb. I remember it well. I bent down and washed it off in the water, and by the time I looked up, one hell of a storm was breaking."

The voices of the women on the dock got louder. Some trawlers were returning from the sea. When they recognized a father, a husband, or a son, they shouted with joy. The rest of the women stood sadly staring into the distance. The woman with the child in her arms stood silently, gazing at the point where the waves formed.

The fisherman returned to his tale. "It was a terrible storm. Our long-boat broke up. That's when my brother died. He didn't even know how to swim. My son and I barely made it to the beach not far from here."

He drank deeply, as if it were his last chance. He brushed droplets off his white beard and sat staring into his empty glass, looking for secrets, or maybe some tenderness.

"I heard your story in the city," I said. "I heard you never went out again, and—"

He broke in. "Did they call us cowards?"

I told him I heard it in a mariners' bar, and that sailors take pleasure in recounting the mysteries and tragedies of the sea. In the diamond glint of the old man's eye, I saw something, hatred, or maybe despair. Rain sluiced down the window and splashed onto the paves below, softening the look of them. I read in his eyes that nothing could keep a sailor from returning to the sea, not fear, not a wife, not a legend. And the rain fell on the mutinous, burgeoning sea.

Most of the trawlers had made it to port by then. Only one vessel was unaccounted for, and only a few women remain on the dock. One of them was holding a frightened child by the hand. Her tired eyes continued to search the distant darkness after most of the others went home with their sailors to the warmth of the hearth where they hung their shirts and trousers to dry and felt protected beneath their husbands. Suddenly thunder exploded overhead, and the rain became a downpour, collapsing umbrellas, deepening the darkness, and striking at the hopes of those who were waiting. Then the dock was empty, occupied only by the storm. The mother with the toddler in her arms came into the tavern. She was soaked and sopping, like wet bread. She was morose and impatient at the same time. The waves broke over the dock.

"Who is she?" I asked the old man, even though I felt I knew.

"The wife of a fisherman who didn't come back," he said.

I was pretty sure I knew, but I didn't ask again. Now the rain was beating like a drum, like a hundred drums on the broad window. In the child's blue eyes, I saw the same diamond glint I'd seen in the old mariner's.

A boy arrived, soaking wet and gasping for air, all excited. He said the last boat was coming in, you could see it from the lookout point. The woman left in a rush, pulling the toddler by the hand, not even bothering to open her umbrella. The old sailor got up and tottered to the door. I followed him. Along the dock under the dark storm, up some slippery stone stairs, and we managed to climb the slope to the chapel and the lookout. Five or six women gathered around an oil lamp and looked out at some invisible point on the wild sea. High on the lookout, the wind whistled through their long hair and whipped their clothes and the branches of trees, while far below the heavy waves crashed against the rocks at the foot of the cliff.

A tiny boat struggled on the swollen sea, looking like a fly in a tumbler of water. Tossed among the waves, sometimes it sank out of sight only to reappear on the surface, seemingly no bigger than a dead insect. The child cried "Mama" and the woman's eyes grew wet, but not with rain or sea spray. The boat inched toward the harbor between waves as dangerous as giant knives.

We all went back down the stone stairs in the dark and the rain. The old man walked glumly by my side.

I asked him, "Do you believe that legend about the seagulls?"

"What's to believe? The sea kills a fisherman who has killed a seagull. But the fisherman who fails to go out because his wife tells him not to, he's not a fisherman. He's nothing."

The women were moving toward the dock, joined by a few men who'd come down from the houses. We went back inside the inn and watched from the window, ordering two gins. In the dim light, they cast the rope from the prow of the trawler and made it fast to the iron bollard. The woman with the child turned abruptly and ran back to her house in the shadows.

"Why didn't she stay to wait for her husband?" I asked.

"My son stayed home a long, long time, but today he went out to the fishing grounds. This morning eight men went out in the trawler, and now seven have come back. My son hasn't."

There was no lessening of the rain. I was thinking that the sea was a deep black mouth with no gulls. The bartender brought our gin in glass tumblers, and the old man's wrinkled fingers carried it immediately to his mouth. Some of the women from the dock went silently to the house of the woman and child. Soon no one could be seen outside the window. The two of us were left alone in the bar, next to the oil lamp.

All the sadness of the sea lay in the old fisherman's eyes as he said to me, "Now tell me why you've come."

IBAN ZALDUA (Donostia, 1966)

I am an historian by training and, at least for now, by profession as well; I teach economic history in Gasteiz, the city where I live.

In 1989 I published my first book, which was written in Spanish, *Veinte cuentos cortitos* (*Twenty Very Short Stories*). Then came books in Basque: *Ipuin euskaldunak* (1999, *Basque Short Stories*, with G. Markuleta), *Gezurrak, gezurrak, gezurrak* (2000, *Lies, Lies, Lies*), *Traizioak* (2001, *Betrayals*), and another in Spanish, *La isla de los antropólogos y otros relatos* (2002, *The Antroplologists' Island and Other Short Stories*). All of these are books of short stories. In children's literature, I wrote *Kea ur gainean* (2002, *Smoke on the Water*), and then a short essay, *Obabatiko tranbia. Zenbait gogoeta azken aldiko euskal literaturaz (1989-2001)* (2002, *The Train from Obaba. Some Refflections on Recent Basque Literature (1989-2001)*), both in Basque.

I consider myself a storyteller; I wouldn't say that stories and novels are opposites, but that they are very different genres. I agree with the writer John Cheever when se says that at the moment of death we tell ourselves a short story, at that moment there's no time for a novel; I think this is an excellent assertion to highlight the intensity of a short story. However, as Augusto Monterroso said, thankfully, what a story is can never be defined; supposedly the art of writing stories has some rules, but the following is the only true rule: precisely, that rules are meant to be broken.

Bibliography

by

IBAN ZALDUA

Translated by Kristin Addis

The alleged terrorist arrested the day before yesterday is in the middle of the room, in an uncomfortable chair, hands and legs tied. In a cold sweat. Suddenly he raises his eyes, and dares to look toward the policeman who tortured him half an hour earlier. The policeman's face is hidden behind a ski mask, and he's reading a book. He doesn't seem to realize the prisoner has woken up, since he doesn't raise his eyes. The alleged terrorist is stunned to recognize the book in the policeman's hands: the same pearly gray cover, the same design, the same title and author. The alleged terrorist has also read this book, not long ago. He doesn't understand how it can be in his torturer's hands. He remembers that he read it with the same passion he now sees in the policeman. He hardly noticed what was going on around him. He never wanted to reach the end of that book.

Policeman 76635-Q's boyfriend gave him the book, a week ago. He loves reading, but doesn't have much time for it. He decided to leave the book at work, to take advantage of the odd free moment and read a few pages. His co-workers laugh at him when they see him take the book from his desk drawer, since they've never seen him so involved. 76635-Q doesn't care. This book is special.

He never wants to reach the end of it. It's the first time this has happened to him.

A.J.C., the policeman's boyfriend, reads quite a bit more than 76635-Q. His work isn't so hectic (he works at the jail), and he has hours on his hands without much to do. He would like to spark this interest in 76635-Q because he loves to talk about books (and about films), but he hasn't had much luck so far. In fact, he didn't know if he was picking a winner with this book, and still doesn't know; they haven't been together since he gave 76635-Q the book. He'll be delighted when he next gets together with the policeman, tomorrow or the next day, and the first thing he hears from him will be how much he likes this book. A.J.C. acquired the book in a search of the 4th cellblock, in a cell they turned inside out. He doesn't remember the name or face of the prisoner whose cell it was, nor whether they found anything there. He just saw the book on a shelf, and since he recognized the author's name, he decided to take it. He doesn't regret it; it's this author's best work, without a doubt.

The prison worker A.J.C. doesn't remember the prisoner in that cell, but Pedro (that was his name) remembers that inspection clearly, as well as the millions he endured before it. To tell the truth, he doesn't mind so much about the book. He never would have managed to finish it anyway, but he kept pictures of his girlfriend among its pages and losing those pictures pisses him off – they were pretty, very colorful, taken in Benidorm and Alicante. In that search, they fucked up his little television set too.

The girlfriend smiling in Pedro's pictures wouldn't care to be known as such; at the most, she would admit to being Pedro's ex-girlfriend. Sara Fuentes hates those months she shared an apartment with Pedro; hates Pedro too, or hated him, she's no longer sure — so much time has passed. Now she lives in her parents' house again, and works in a flower shop, half-days. She no longer uses heroin, and therefore no longer has to commit petty theft to buy it. Sara has completely forgotten the book she left behind when she left Pedro, as well as a number of other things she abandoned in the apartment. She stole it from the city library, and in fact, policeman 76635-Q just now realizes this when he sees the library's seal on the lower right-hand corner of page III (later he'll realize the same seal also appears on pages 2II and 3II). Sara tried to sell the book a couple times at the Sunday market in the new plaza, but no luck. The books by Michael Crichton and Vázquez Figuero that she stole from the Corte Inglés, on the other hand, they couldn't buy fast enough.

When the book arrived at the library, Alizia Fernández de Larrea catalogued it and put the seal on pages III, 2II and 3II; also on the first page, but Sara ripped out that whole page before trying to sell the book. When Alizia was putting the seal in it, she decided she would read the book; she had already had the chance to skim the beginning, and she liked it. But she didn't have time to carry out her plan. One afternoon, as she was driving home, a bomb went off, intended for the Civil Guard patrol car behind her. The Civil Guards came out fine, but Alizia was severely injured, and died in the hospital five hours later.

Among other things, they want a confession to having taken part in this attack from the alleged terrorist in the middle of the room, in an uncomfortable chair, hands and legs tied and in a cold sweat. The alleged terrorist, on the other hand, has forgotten all the endless questions they asked, and the book the policeman is reading is the only thing in his mind. He liked that book so much. With something like a smile, he remembers he decided to buy it because his name and the author's are the same. And because he had to wait an entire morning sitting next to the picture window in that cafe. An antidote for boredom.

As he thinks these thoughts, policeman 76635-Q closes the book, and,

half-heartedly, starts to rise.

Invisible Friend

by

IBAN ZALDUA

Translated by Kristin Addis

When I was a kid, I had an invisible friend. His name was Tommy. He had brown hair and he was short, quite chubby, reserved. He always wore shorts, winter or summer. We played together all the time — at home, at school, in the park, on the beach, everywhere. When my mother gets nostalgic and starts reminiscing out loud about my childhood, she usually says I was a loner of a kid. Mostly I let it go, but every once in a while I object: "How can you say I was such a loner, Mom? Don't you remember the time Tommy and I filled the house with frogs? Or what about the night when we spotlighted the couples making out on the benches on the walk? The flashlight was Tommy's." Even though she shakes her head gently, she surely must remember that night, since she came back from the movies with my father to find two cops watching over me, called to the scene by one of those irate lovers. Tommy, the fox, managed to escape, who knows how.

Until we turned twelve, we were inseparable. Then I started to grow away from Tommy; Alex had become my best friend. It's one of the mysteries of childhood. From one day to the next, someone who was a god to you ceases to be interesting and there's not a thing he can do about it; even worse, everything he does to stay friends seems more and more hateful. That's what happened to Tommy.

Tommy didn't want to give up, but when he saw that his efforts were in vain, he turned on me. At recess, when no one was looking, he would push me down, and I went home every day covered in bruises. My teachers told my parents I was falling down by myself, and no one believed me when I blamed Tommy. He would come into my bedroom at night and leave a bloodbath of red ink across my homework. He appeared to me in nightmares; I gave up sleeping. But the worst was what happened with Alex. One day Tommy came to me in the park. "Your little friend has cancer," he said. Six months later they told us Alex had leukemia. He never came back to school.

In the following years I went from psychiatrist to psychiatrist, and Tommy's visits gradually became less frequent until he disappeared completely. The doctors were happy; I had learned to refer to Tommy as my "invisible friend." From then on, I was calmer at least.

Until today. I'm always at home when my son comes home from school. "What have you got there, Alex?" I asked him. "Tommy gave it to me, Dad," and he showed me the flashlight, "He said he'd teach me a cool game with it."

PERMISSIONS